Her fire alarm blared.

Maggie shot up in bed and stared at the darkness surrounding her, trying to orient herself to the sound blasting the stillness.

A pounding at her front door propelled her from her bed. She raced from the room and in the hallway met a wall of smoke pouring from her office. She headed for the front door.

Suddenly it burst open, and Kane hurried into her apartment, his chest rising and falling rapidly.

"I called the fire department. Get out now."

Maggie grabbed Kane's arm as he passed her. "Where are you going? Aren't you leaving, too?"

"I have to try to stop the fire."

She couldn't let him do it alone. "Then I'm going with you."

Books by Margaret Daley

Love Inspired Suspense

Hearts on the Line
Heart of the Amazon
So Dark the Night
Vanished
Buried Secrets
Don't Look Back
Forsaken Canyon
What Sarah Saw
Poisoned Secrets

Love Inspired

The Power of Love
Family for Keeps
Sadie's Hero
The Courage to Dream
What the Heart Knows
A Family for Tory
*Gold in the Fire
*A Mother for Cindy
*Light in the Storm
The Cinderella Plan
*When Dreams Come True
*Tidings of Joy
**Once Upon a Family
**Heart of the Family
**Family Ever After

*The Ladies of
   Sweetwater Lake
**Fostered by Love

MARGARET DALEY

feels she has been blessed. She has been married more than thirty years to her husband, Mike, whom she met in college. He is a terrific support and her best friend. They have one son, Shaun. Margaret has been writing for many years and loves to tell a story. When she was a little girl, she would play with her dolls and make up stories about their lives. Now she writes these stories down. She especially enjoys weaving stories about families and how faith in God can sustain a person when things get tough. When she isn't writing, she is fortunate to be a teacher for students with special needs. Margaret has taught for over twenty years and loves working with her students. She has also been a Special Olympics coach and participated in many sports with her students.

POISONED SECRETS

Margaret Daley

Steeple
Hill®

Published by Steeple Hill Books™

STEEPLE HILL BOOKS

Steeple Hill®

Recycling programs
for this product may
not exist in your area.

ISBN-13: 978-0-373-44329-1
ISBN-10:   0-373-44329-3

POISONED SECRETS

Beloved, if God so loved us,
we ought to also love one another.
—*1 John* 4:11

To the Lord, without You this wouldn't be possible.

ONE

A loud thud from the apartment above made Kane McDowell flinch and sit straight up in the lounger.

"What was that?" Edwina Bacon asked, putting her teacup down on the table next to her.

Kane's gaze riveted to the ceiling of Edwina's place. "Maybe Henry dropped something."

"I don't know. He didn't look well tonight when I saw him go upstairs. That's the second strange sound I've heard coming from the apartment above. What if he fell and hurt himself?"

"You worry too much about the tenants, Edwina. Henry's certainly capable of taking care of himself." His words didn't erase the worry on the elderly woman's face. Kane pushed to his feet. "But if it will make you feel better, I'll go upstairs and check."

"Oh, thank you. I wouldn't want anything to happen to someone here. Even Henry."

"You read too many mysteries," Kane said as he headed for the foyer of the apartment building he owned.

Kane's leg ached as he mounted the stairs to the second floor of the converted mansion. He'd overdone it today. Covering the short distance to apartment 2A, he knocked. He waited a minute and then rang the bell. Nothing.

Henry Payne sometimes was out late. But if that were the case, then what made the crashing sound? Reluctantly Kane dug into his pocket for the master key. He fit it into the lock and turned it, but the door was already unlocked.

Alarmed, he thrust the door open, every skill he'd learned in the military activated. The overpowering odors of cigars and lemon polish assailed his nostrils. The complete chaos scattered about this usually tidy, orderly place put Kane on alert. This definitely wasn't a heart attack. Cautiously he moved into the lighted living area, listening for any sounds coming from the rest of the apartment. Silence greeted him.

"Henry," he called out while scanning the room where every book the man owned, which had to be hundreds, seemed to be tossed on the floor. Drawer contents littered the beige area rug, and all the cabinets were emptied. The crunch of glass beneath his feet drew his glance. The mirror over the table in the small entryway lay on the hardwood floor in shattered pieces. Probably the crash Edwina heard.

Maybe Henry's gone.

Or maybe not.

Coveting his own privacy, Kane hated invading another's, but it was obvious something had gone terribly wrong here. He headed down the short hallway to investigate the two bedrooms. Each one was as neat and tidy as he knew Henry to be.

Back in the living room, Kane limped toward the kitchen to check out the rest of the place. When he swung the door open, the stench of blood—something he would never forget from his time in Iraq—accosted him. The cool breeze from an open window that led to the balcony chilled the room. As Kane inched forward, the door swung closed. The sound of its swish drew his attention behind him. He froze.

On the floor in a crimson pool lay Henry, his dark eyes staring at the ceiling, his arm flung out at an odd angle, a patch of light blue fabric clutched in his hand.

TWO

Maggie Ridgeway stared at the Twin Oaks Apartments. The converted late nineteenth century mansion's brick was painted a flesh tone, and its trim and shutters a snowy white. Three stories tall with a porch that ran almost the full length of its front, the building dominated the spacious yard with multi-colored spring flowers blooming in the well-tended beds. Two massive oaks stood sentinel. A stained glass window with a pastoral scene was above the entrance, and below it were double, dark brown doors with beveled glass.

Finally!

She was here and intended to stay.

Maggie marched up the stairs to find the manager and secure the vacant apartment before someone else did. A friend she worked with at the hospital told her a vacancy in this building was rare and didn't last long. Afraid she'd never get the opportunity, she was ready to pounce on the opening she'd been anxiously waiting several months for since moving to Seven Oaks, Kentucky.

She stepped into the spacious foyer, a wide staircase directly in front of her sweeping up to the second floor. A gleaming chandelier hung from the ceiling, and a huge round cherry table with a bouquet of expensive silk flowers in a crystal vase sat under the light, adding a splash of vivid colors to the entrance. An ornate Persian rug, predominantly navy-blue and maroon, covered the marble floor in the center, giving off a warm, cozy feeling.

Surveying the first floor, she found the door with a brass plaque with the word *manager* engraved on it. She covered the short distance to the apartment and rang the bell.

"She's not home," a child's voice said behind her.

Maggie turned around and saw a thin boy with brown hair standing on the staircase, gripping the wooden balustrade. Her heart lurched at the sight of him. Only a few yards away. Staring into his dark eyes, she felt as though she were staring into her own. Kenny! The thought made her take a step back until she pressed up against the manager's door.

She'd imagined meeting and talking to him for the first time. But now no words would come to mind. Emotions, held at bay, crashed down on her. Emptiness, anger, elation, all swirling around in her, made a knot form in her stomach.

"Ma'am, are you all right?" His freckled face scrunched up into a worried look.

Maggie continued to peer at the boy. Her smile faltered while her heartbeat began to hammer against her rib cage. She'd told herself this would happen and thought she'd prepared herself for it.

The child shifted, alarm flittering across his features. "Lady?"

With her pulse thundering in her ears, she finally replied, "I want to rent the vacant apartment. Do you know when the manager will be back?" Amazingly her voice didn't quaver although her hands did. She clutched her purse straps to keep the trembling under control.

Besides his eyes, his hair's the same shade of brown as mine. And I used to have freckles the way he does. She swallowed the lump in her throat. *I should leave. Let it go.* She rubbed her damp palms together, fighting the urge to scrap her plan.

"She'll probably be gone for another hour or so." The child moved forward. "Uncle Kane's here, though."

"Uncle?" Maggie pushed herself away from the door and moved several paces toward the eleven-year-old boy. Her legs quaked.

"Well, he's not really my uncle, but I call him that. He owns the building. He can help you."

"Where is he?"

He jerked his thumb toward a door down the hall at the back of the building. "In his shop downstairs." Gesturing with his hand, he spun around on his heel. "C'mon. I'll show you."

"I'm Maggie Ridgeway. What's your name?" she asked although she was ninety-nine percent sure she already knew it.

"Kenny Pennington."

Even though she'd expected him to say that, the name brought an added joy to her. That feeling tangled with the others—uncertainty, even anger—firming in her mind told her she had to continue with her plan. She'd dreamed about this moment for too long to turn back now.

The sound of sandpaper sliding over wood filled the workroom. The scent of sawdust and linseed oil peppered the air. Repeatedly Kane McDowell ran the block along the groove in the piece of furniture, smoothing the rough texture.

The rhythmic motion of the sanding—back and forth—relaxed Kane, his thoughts wandering as his hands automatically repeated the action. The tension slipped from his shoulders and neck while he proceeded from one chair leg to the next. As the tautness eased completely from his body, his awareness of his surroundings faded, too. The movement of his arm was hypnotic, the gritty sound almost soothing.

The memory came unexpectedly as it so often did. His thoughts were at peace one second, and the next, he flinched, stopped his sanding and closed his eyes as though that could shut it out. It never did…

"I can't do it. I thought I could. I don't want to marry you anymore. I'm moving to Dallas, Kane." Ruth indicated the luggage at the door.

He stood in his parents' living room, having been at their home for the past month to continue his convalescence after his injury in Iraq. Last week his fiancée had come to help nurse him back to full health. Now she was leaving him.

At the door she paused and looked back at him. *"I need a whole man. I tried. I really did. You aren't the same person you were when you went to war."* Her gaze swept down his length, his body propped up by crutches, his left leg gone from just below the knee dangling uselessly next to his good one…

Kane shook his head as if he could physically drive the memory from his thoughts. The sanding block fell from his hand, thumping to the concrete, its sound reverberating through his mind. Sweat dripped into his eyes, stinging them.

A knock jarred the silence.

"Not now," he muttered, swiping his forehead with the back of his hand. He needed to escape; he didn't want to see anyone.

Another knock echoed through his workshop.

Trapped.

Maggie raised her hand one final time to rap on the door when it suddenly opened. She stared into the face of a man who didn't look too happy to see her. His dark expression didn't soften as she cleared her throat and said, "I came about renting your apartment."

The man's hard gaze bore into her. The taut set of his body, his grip on the door handle, conveyed tension. Then his attention fixed on Kenny, and the owner's stiff stance melted, the frown wiped away to be replaced with an expression just short of a smile.

Kenny looked at Maggie. "Miss Edwina's at church so I brought her down here to see you."

The man who owned the apartment building finally smiled— a fully fledged one that lit his whole face and dimpled his cheeks. "I'll take it from here, Kenny. Thanks."

The boy spun around and raced up the stairs. The second he disappeared the strain returned to the owner's face, his gaze directed at her.

Suddenly the small hallway in the basement closed in on Maggie. She glanced around, noting three other doors, one of them leading outside. A bank of windows on each side of it afforded a view of the back of the building and a glimpse of the lake beyond.

"Dale Franklin told me there was an apartment in your building for rent. He was supposed to call you about me coming to see the place."

The man, over six feet tall, eased his grip on the door and relaxed against it. "Edwina Bacon, my manager, must have talked with Dale. I don't usually handle anything having to do with the apartment building."

"Then should I wait for her to return?"

"Suit yourself, but frankly I'm surprised you'd want to rent it. I haven't even put an advertisement in the paper yet. Not sure I am for a while. Are you aware of what happened in it a few weeks back? The police just released it a couple of days ago."

Yes, she'd known that and had barely been able to wait the few days before coming to see about the apartment. The headlines that had occupied the newspaper for a week flashed into her thoughts, bringing forth a momentary surge of anxiety until she remembered the reason she wanted to live here.

"Yes, but I'm living in a dorm connected with the hospital right now. I need a more permanent place to live, and there are few available in Seven Oaks at this time of year with the university in full swing."

"Hospital? Are you a nurse?"

"No, a speech therapist, Mr.—"

"Kane McDowell."

Before her courage totally failed her, she said, "I didn't want anyone else to get the apartment, so I took some time off from work to come here. I really need a place to live. My privacy means a lot to me, and I have none where I'm living right now." His eyes lit with understanding. "May I look at the apartment?"

"Give me a moment, and I'll show it to you."

He left her standing by the door while he sauntered to the sink. His chest, covered by a white T-shirt, revealed his wide expanse of muscles. His faded jeans hugged slim hips and the long legs of a runner.

He splashed water on his face, then reached for a towel. His damp black hair curled at his nape in ringlets as he dried it. When he retrieved his blue short-sleeve polo shirt from an unfinished chair and shrugged into it, his sheer male power transfixed her. He was in top physical condition.

As he faced her, she hastily pretended an interest in the far wall with a myriad of tools hanging on it, fighting the heat of a blush that suffused her cheeks. "You're a carpenter?"

"Some of the time."

"And the other times?" Finally she looked into his slate-gray eyes and wished she hadn't. They were startling against the darkness of his features, their color like polished pewter.

"I'm the admissions director at the university." He walked past her into the hallway. "I'll show you the apartment now."

As she followed him, she got the distinct impression that was all the chitchat she would get out of the man.

"The apartment is on the second floor, Miss—" He peered back at her, snaring her within his flintlike gaze.

"Maggie Ridgeway."

His guarded look conveyed the message: stay away. The silent statement pulsated in the air between them, intriguing her, tempting her. She knew all the signs of someone who kept himself apart from others. She was a master at it. He could do nothing she hadn't done herself at some time in her past.

As she mounted the staircase to the second floor, she firmed her determination. She couldn't afford to be side-tracked. *Which one is it?* she thought as she passed a closed door. "How many apartments are in this building?"

"Six on three floors. I occupy the basement." He unlocked apartment 2A and pushed the door open. "As you can see, they're big. I have three families in my building. Some furniture comes with the apartment if you want to use it."

"It'll just be me, and yes, the furniture would be appreciated."

She entered the living room and surveyed the oblong configuration with a marble fireplace on the outer wall, a brass screen across its front. The carved mantel would be a perfect place to set family pictures. But who would be in those photo frames? The question came unbidden into her mind.

"I just finished having the place cleaned," Mr. McDowell said, thankfully pulling her attention from the answer to that question.

A shiver skipped down her spine. She refused to think about Henry Payne, who had been murdered in the kitchen according to the news. A murder yet unsolved. Instead, she let her gaze roam over the neat room with a beige leather couch, a coffee table and two navy and beige plaid wing chairs with a table made of a rich cherry wood between them. A bank of built-in bookcases, all empty, ran the length of one wall. On another were two large floor-to-ceiling windows flanking the fireplace, which offered a view of the neighbor's house, twenty yards away, and the barest glimpse of the lake behind the house. The walls painted maroon gave a feeling of cozy warmth that completely contradicted what had happened in the apartment recently.

"I'll take it. When can I move in?"

"Immediately, if you want." Puzzled, he cocked his head to the side. "Wouldn't you like to look at the rest of it first?"

"No, this is fine. It's close to Seven Oaks Hospital and in a nice neighborhood. As I mentioned before, there aren't too many places available at this time of year."

When she shifted her attention to Kane McDowell, his eyes narrowed on her for an uncomfortable moment as if he were delving into her mind to see what was really behind her desire to live in his apartment building, especially in a place where tragedy had occurred. She schooled her features into a neutral expression, determined not to reveal her hidden motive.

"Normally I have a person fill out an application and then I run a credit check, but if Edwina has gotten a recommendation from Dale, then I'll lease it to you. I require first and last months' rent."

She released the breath she held slowly, covering the space between them and holding out her hand. "It's a deal, Mr. McDowell."

The rough feel of his hand warmed hers. When he let go and stepped out into the hallway, the lingering effect of his touch streaked up her arm, jolting her heart to beat faster. Maggie clenched her hands together to still the slight tremor. This man did strange things to her insides, and this certainly wasn't a time in her life to pursue an attraction. She'd come to Seven Oaks for only one thing. She couldn't let anything stand in the way of her mission.

"I'll get a lease, and you can sign it." Kane retraced his steps to the basement.

"That's great. I'd like to move in as soon as possible."
Maggie hurried to keep up with him.

Unlocking a door across from his workshop, he motioned
for her to enter his apartment. When she stepped inside, the
comfortable-looking living room with large windows offering
a view of the lake surprised her. After only a short time in his
presence, she had been sure his place would be dark and stark
like the man. But because the apartment building sat on a hill
that sloped to the lake, the basement wasn't totally below
ground. The back half was opened to the sprawling yard with
oaks, maples and elms dotting its terrain down to the water.

"Have a seat while I get a lease. I'm sure I have one around
here somewhere," he said and walked toward a hallway.

Restless, she paced. *Maybe I should leave the past alone.
Maybe I should go back to St. Louis and forget. Maybe—no, I
can't walk away now. This wouldn't have been possible without
You. I know it in here.* She tapped her chest over her heart. *Lord,
it's finally happening after all these years. Thank You.*

Every nerve ending alert, Maggie stopped pacing and
rotated toward Kane who moved into the room, a paper in his
hand. Their gazes locked. Her lungs constricted at the power
emanating from him.

Suddenly, he broke eye contact and crossed the room. "The
rent's due on the first. There's to be no loud music or noise
after ten. Pets are allowed so long as they're small and not dis-
ruptive to the other tenants. Oh, and trash is picked up every
Tuesday and Friday." He laid the lease on the coffee table with
the apartment key next to it. "Any questions?"

"No." Matching his strictly business demeanor, she sat on
the rust-colored couch, noted the amount of the rent, then
signed her name on the lease.

He retrieved the lease. "This is contingent on the fact Dale
gives you a glowing recommendation."

"He will."

"Tomorrow's okay to move in, but I still have a few things to do to the apartment. That's one of the reasons I took some vacation time."

"Fine. I'll be working tomorrow morning, so I won't be here till the afternoon."

"I'll try to be out of the way by two." He started for his door. "You can give me the rent then, and I'll give you a copy of the signed lease. I'll also introduce you to Edwina tomorrow. She'll handle everything after that."

Maggie rifled through her oversize purse and withdrew her checkbook. "Let me pay now. One less thing to handle later." As she filled out the check, she asked in a casual voice, "Who else besides Edwina Bacon lives here?"

"On the first floor across from Edwina there's the Sellman family with a set of twins. The Penningtons live across from you. You've already met Kenny Pennington. Upstairs from you there's Kyra Williams with her son, Sean, and lastly Edwina's sister Ann and her husband, Marcus Quinn." He walked toward the front door and opened it. "If there's nothing else, I'll see you tomorrow afternoon."

Effectively dismissed, Maggie escaped into the hallway and started for the stairs. *What am I doing here?* Panic seized her.

Father, give me the strength to see this through to the end, whatever that may be. Give me the strength to do the right thing when dealing with the woman who gave me up at birth.

The box must weigh a ton! Maggie tried to shift the weight some as she stopped halfway up the stairs to her new apartment, but she lost what grip she had. The box crashed to the step in front of her. The sound of glass breaking echoed through the quiet.

"Can I help?" Kenny asked as he came up behind her.

Still unaccustomed to having her half brother so near, Maggie tensed for a few seconds before forcing herself to relax and smile. "I don't think anyone can help now. I think Grandma Ridgeway's glassware is gone." She plopped down on the step, placing her elbows on her knees and resting her chin in her palms.

"Maybe it's not so bad." The brown-haired boy peered into the container and whistled.

She slanted a look at him. "That bad?"

"Yep, 'fraid so." He sat down next to her. "You're moving into the apartment across from us. Uncle Kane told me."

"I'm glad we're neighbors." She had always wanted siblings and now she was sitting not inches from her half brother. The moment awed her, and yet she wasn't sure what to do about it. She'd gone twenty-eight years without any experience on how to relate to a younger brother.

The child's expression showed concern. "Will your grandma be too upset?"

"Nope," she murmured around the lump in her throat. *Where do I begin getting to know my brother?*

"I know if I'd done something like that, my grandma woulda been upset *big-time*. And my mom would be crying by now. Once she broke a dish my grandma gave her and she cried. Told me family was important to her."

His words stole her breath. Her lungs burned as she tried to drag air into them. "Your mother's right." *And she robbed me of mine.* She fought the tears that now gathered in her throat in order to ask, "Would you like to help me finish unloading my car? I'll pay you."

"Sure!" Kenny beamed. "Mom isn't gonna be home for a while. I could use the money—that's if you don't mind Ashley tagging along."

"Fine. Is she your sister?" She knew the answer, but it

didn't stop the feeling of too much happening too fast and the need to slow down.

"My baby sister." His face screwed up into a frown as though he'd just taken a spoonful of distasteful medicine.

"Tell you what." Maggie lifted the box, grimacing when she heard the broken glass clinking. "I'll take this to my apartment while you get Ashley. Then we'll head to my car."

Hurrying up the stairs, she needed to put some distance between herself and Kenny before she cried in front of him. She'd dreamed of getting to know her family for a long time— ever since she had learned her birth mother had one—but she'd never dreamed of the rush of excitement that she felt, the anxiety that caused a pressure in her chest, the tug of emotions that ripped through her gut. And the overriding thought that she'd missed so many years of this child's life, as well as Ashley's.

At the top of the stairs she paused to catch her breath, to swallow the tears. She looked down at Kenny, who waved and smiled. She returned his grin, resisting the urge to rush down the steps and hug the boy.

I have to take it slow and easy.

Outside her apartment door, she slipped the key into the lock. Surprised it was already unlocked, she tensed, her mind flooded with pictures she'd seen on the nightly news when Henry Payne had been found murdered in this very place.

Cautiously, ready instantly to flee, she eased the door open and peered into the living room. Kane McDowell had said he would be gone by two, and it was well past that time. "Anyone in here?"

"Just me." Kane came into the living room from the kitchen. *Where the murder occurred.* She could do this. She hadn't lived in the town long and certainly didn't have anyone mad enough at her to kill her.

"For a second there, I had visions of tossing this box and hightailing it down the stairs. Not an especially dignified start in my new home." She managed to strike a relaxed pose against the doorjamb.

The sides of his mouth curled upward. "I have your garbage disposal fixed—I think. If this doesn't work, I'll have to replace it."

Stepping closer, his scent of pine engulfing her, he took the box from her. Her mouth went dry. Her reaction to Kane was as strong as the day before. After meeting Kenny, she realized she would have little emotional energy left after dealing with the Penningtons to pursue any other kind of relationship.

"That was beginning to look awfully heavy. Where do you want it?"

"Probably the trash." When his forehead creased in question, she continued, "I dropped it on the stairs. That doesn't sit too well with glass. I guess I'd better check it, though, to see if anything is salvageable."

"How much do you have to carry in today?"

"A carload. I do have several pieces of furniture in storage that I'll move here later when I'm settled." Those pieces were the only connection she had to her adoptive father. A rush of sadness washed over her at the thought of never seeing him again. Such a good man.

Kane glanced at the box. "I can lend you a hand with your unloading."

"That's great." Although a deep ache had burrowed into her heart, she arranged her features into a smile. "I have one helper, but truthfully I wasn't sure how I was going to get some of the larger items up those stairs."

"Who's helping you?"

"Kenny." Maggie started to ask some questions about him and Ashley when the two children appeared in the doorway.

Kenny grinned while Ashley hid behind her big brother, peeping around him with her thumb in her mouth.

Maggie wanted more than anything to scoop both children up in her arms and hug them tightly. She might never be able to do that; she might always be no more than the lady who lived across the hall. The realization cut deeply.

"Are you all ready to work?" Maggie asked, putting a firm lid down on her volatile emotions.

Kenny nodded while Ashley stared at the floor.

"I'll pay you, too, Ashley." Maggie stepped to the side to get a better view of her little sister.

The child ducked behind Kenny even more, concealing her face from Maggie. A knifelike pain sliced through her heart. Her half sister wasn't playing hide-and-seek; she was hiding—from her. Ashley's actions only reinforced the fact that Maggie was a stranger to her own family.

"She's an old scaredy-cat. She'll probably just watch. That's all she ever does." Kenny frowned at his baby sister.

"That's okay." Whirling around, Maggie headed out into the hallway, needing fresh air desperately.

A bond with Ashley formed in the moment Maggie watched her little sister trudge out of the apartment behind Kenny, her gaze glued to the floor, her thumb in her mouth. She knew the frightened feelings Ashley experienced around new people because she had been there herself until one day she'd decided she couldn't spend her life locked up inside of herself and did something about it. She'd forced herself out of her shell but only so far. Still craving solitude, she preferred watching people from a distance, but it was suddenly very important to help Ashley. Maggie prayed the child would let her.

Descending the staircase, Maggie suppressed a flash of anger. All her life she'd wanted a large family, full of brothers and sisters, laughter and love. Now she was faced with two children who regarded her as a stranger and would never know her as their big sister since she had no intention of saying anything about who she was. She only wanted to get to know them from afar, learn about them from her observations. Why give her birth mother a second chance to reject her? She'd had enough of that in her life.

The next afternoon after Edwina Bacon paid her a visit with a welcome gift of banana nut bread, Maggie sat at her kitchen table downing a large glass of iced tea, relishing the cool liquid as she took a break from unpacking. Every muscle in her body ached. She rolled her shoulders, refusing to look at the spot where Henry Payne's body had been. There wasn't a trace of blood on the beige tile because it was brand new, shining in the sunlight streaming through the bay window that overlooked the lake and yard.

Back to work. Finishing her drink, she pushed to her feet and put her glass in the sink. When she started for the living room, a pounding at her front door interrupted her trek to the nearest box. Instead, she answered the urgency in the knock.

"School's out already?" Maggie asked as she took in the sight of Kenny. Then she noticed the frantic look in his eyes. "What's wrong?"

"Come quick. It's Ashley. She can't breathe."

In a space of a heartbeat, Maggie reacted to Kenny's words. She hastened across the hall to the Pennington's open front door, following the boy into the apartment. Ashley stood near the dining room table, clutching her throat, trying desperately to draw air into her lungs, her eyes wide with fear. The bluish tint to Ashley's skin alarmed Maggie. She must have something in her throat. For a few seconds, terror held her immobile until her emergency training kicked in.

Maggie raced to the little girl and encircled her torso. *Please, dear God, not Ashley. I can't lose her now.*

Clasping a fisted hand under the child's rib cage, Maggie pressed upward in four quick thrusts. Relief trembled through her when she saw a peanut pop out of the girl's mouth. Ashley coughed, then began to breathe again.

Maggie gently laid the child on the floor, then hugged Ashley to her. The sound of Maggie's heart beating roared in her ears as she struggled to control the quaking of her body. She had to remain calm, but for the life of her, she wasn't sure how she would. She had almost lost her sister, and she had just found her.

"Are you all right?" Maggie asked when she thought her voice would work.

Ashley's shudder rippled along Maggie's body. The child nodded but kept her arms locked about Maggie while dragging in deep breaths. She stroked the little girl's long brown hair and thanked the Lord.

"You'll be okay now," Maggie whispered as much to reassure herself as her sister. Never in her life had she felt so scared as she had when she had seen Ashley unable to suck in air.

The five-year-old sobbed against Maggie's chest, tremor after tremor passing through her small body into hers. "I—I couldn't—breathe."

"I know, honey." Her arms around Ashley tightened as though Maggie could absorb the child's fear and wipe from her mind the past few minutes. What if she hadn't been here to help? She clung tighter to the child.

"What happened?" Kane asked from the doorway.

"Maggie saved Ashley's life," Kenny said, his face still registering his own fear and panic. "She was blue!"

Maggie looked up at Kane, his gaze ensnaring hers. "She'll be all right now. A peanut went down the wrong way."

For a brief moment distress lined his face until Kane visibly took command of his emotions. He glanced from Maggie to Ashley. Crossing the room, he took the child into his arms. The small girl wrapped herself against him as he held her cradled to him, his eyes soft with concern, a smile of reassurance on his face.

"Uncle Kane, I tried to. Really I tried." Ashley hiccupped between her words, tears cascading down her cheeks.

An ashen cast to his skin sharpened the hard planes of his face. "Shh," Kane whispered while he held Ashley in his arms. "I won't let anything else happen to you."

He walked down the hallway toward the bedrooms and disappeared inside one. Maggie stood. All strength flowed from her legs. She clutched a dining room chair to steady herself, trying to assimilate what had just taken place.

"Kenny! What's going on in here?"

Both Maggie and Kenny turned at the sound of the woman's voice. Maggie felt paralyzed, staring at the woman who had given birth to her. In that instant when their gazes touched, time came to a standstill for Maggie. She didn't have to be introduced to Victoria Pennington to know the woman standing inside the doorway was her birth mother. She was a stranger, yet she was familiar at the same time. Maggie experienced the most disconcerting feeling.

"Who is this woman, Kenny? You know my rule. No one is allowed in this apartment when I'm gone." Victoria's gaze swung from Kenny to Maggie. Victoria placed her hands on her son's shoulders, her stance protective, her expression accusing as she continued to scrutinize Maggie, stranger to stranger.

Don't you recognize me? Don't you know who I am?

Maggie pushed away from the chair holding her up, a taut band about her chest making each breath difficult. "I'm your new neighbor, Maggie Ridgeway." The words came out in a whisper, her mouth parched. It took all her strength to remain standing a few feet from Victoria Pennington and not shout the truth. Maggie wanted to run; she felt as if her carefully thought-out plan was blowing up in her face, leaving fragments behind to slice her composure to shreds.

"Kenny, that still doesn't excuse you from breaking an important rule," the woman said in a softer tone.

Maggie backed away, beads of sweat coating her brow. She needed to leave before she hyperventilated.

"She saved Ashley's life. She wasn't breathing—"

"What? Where's Ashley?"

"In her room with Uncle Kane," Kenny answered.

Victoria rushed down the hall as Kane came out of Ashley's bedroom. "Vicky, she's okay. She's sleeping now."

With hands clenched at her sides, fingernails digging into her palms, Maggie took another step toward the door, the air charged with intense emotions that demanded she feel something other than indignation. But at this moment she couldn't deny the anger deep in her heart.

While Kane briefly explained what happened, Vicky peered into the room and sighed. "She fell asleep the minute I put her down."

"I should have been here. I got held up at the office. The police came again to the campus to question everyone who knew Henry."

"Yeah, I know. They talked with me." Kane shot Kenny a look.

Vicky closed her daughter's bedroom door and headed toward the living area with Kane. "I wish I didn't have to work. Then that wouldn't have happened."

"It could have happened with you sitting right here."

"John and I are so lucky to have you here. You're like a member of the family. I miss not living near mine."

Maggie felt as if she had been slapped in the face. To them she was an outsider. *But I belong.* She bit the inside of her mouth to keep from shouting the truth. The realization that the words she had no intention of saying had been on the tip of her tongue sent alarm through her.

Kane nodded toward Maggie. "Thankfully Maggie was home to help Kenny."

"I'm sorry about the earlier reception. As you may have gathered by now, I'm Kenny and Ashley's mother, Vicky Pennington. Thanks for saving," her voice faltered for a few seconds before she swallowed hard and finished, "my little girl."

My little girl. But I am also. Lord, I can't do this.

Both Kane and Vicky waited for a response. Maggie fought down the panic surfacing. She needed to escape, retreat to her apartment and regroup.

"I'm glad I was here to help out," Maggie finally said, her throat closing about the words. Her anger swelled to the surface, her fingernails cutting deeper into her palms. *Why did you give me up?* She was afraid to say anything for fear that question would tumble out.

"I helped Maggie move in yesterday," Kenny said, breaking the awkward moment of silence. "She paid me ten dollars!" He took the money out of his pocket and waved it in the air.

Vicky shifted her attention to her son. "Ten dollars?"

Envy, doubt and anger constricted Maggie's stomach. She prayed none of her confused feelings were showing on her face. As Kenny and Vicky talked, Maggie saw her chance to escape. She took the few steps to the entrance and fled into the hallway.

Her gaze fastened on her door, she headed for it. The sound of the one behind her closing relaxed some of the tension in her until she heard Kane say, "Are you all right?"

"Great," she murmured and thrust open her door. *Safe.*

She turned to close it, but Kane had already slipped inside her apartment. She rotated away from his probing gaze. It was bad enough she felt this seesawing between anger and hurt. She certainly didn't want him to see it in her expression.

The sight of the disarray and stacked boxes accentuated her loneliness, a sense of abandonment. She hadn't been prepared for this tangle of confusion twisting her stomach. In St. Louis she had thought she could handle this objectively as she did most things in her life. Wrong. There was nothing objective about this situation.

"Maggie?"

The sound of her front door finally being closed echoed through the apartment—her home now, hundreds of miles away from anything familiar. *Why did I do this? Why couldn't I be happy not ever knowing why my mother gave me up, what my heritage is? Lord, why do I have two mothers who don't really want me?* She desperately sought the strength she always gained when she turned to God for reassurance and comfort.

"Maggie, you aren't all right." Kane touched her hand, sending a bolt of recognition up her arm.

His nearness further eroded her self-confidence, making herself doubt her sanity for even considering this move. She'd gone through life insulating herself from others, and suddenly the walls were crumbling, her usual defenses no longer working. She stepped away, needing to put some distance between them.

His worried expression prompted her to say, "I'm fine. Why do you ask?" None of the nonchalance she wanted to project came across. She held herself so taut that her body ached.

"Oh, I don't know. Maybe it was the pale tone to your skin or the fact you didn't even tell Kenny and Vicky goodbye."

Feigning an interest in an open box, she lifted her shoulders in a shrug. "It isn't every day I save someone's life."

"True. But my gut instinct tells me something else is going on here."

She picked up a book and flipped through it as though she hadn't a care in the world. "What possibly could be going on?" When she thought she had herself under control, she faced him.

He studied her, that piercing gaze of his roaming over her as though he could read her innermost thoughts. She prayed he couldn't because after that scene in the Penningtons' apartment she didn't know if she could go ahead with her quest. She wanted answers, not a relationship with her birth mother. She'd already had one with her adoptive mother that hadn't turned out well. Why subject herself to another?

But still, there were blank holes in her family history she wanted filled. Could she form a friendship with the woman across the hall and discover the answers without disrupting anyone's lives, especially Kenny's and Ashley's?

Shaking his head, Kane massaged the back of his neck. "You know I usually make it a habit to stay out of other people's business."

"Safer, isn't it?"

The intensity in his eyes trapped her. "Yes. Much safer."

For a long moment she stared at him. She glimpsed his vulnerability, a flash of pain, and that touched her battered heart. She wished she could deny his potent effect on her, but she couldn't. She wished she could deny the spark of interest she sensed in his eyes before he veiled it, but she couldn't. Just as she couldn't give up her quest when she was so close to finding some answers.

They both had their secrets. The barrier he had placed around his emotions was strong, possibly impregnable, and she had never been good at tearing down another's defenses because she couldn't get past her own, fortified from years of rejection.

She averted her gaze. "Did you take care of everything in here yesterday?" That ought to be a safe enough subject. His visual assault still tingled up her body. She kept her eyes fixed on a spot across the room.

He moved toward the front door. "I believe everything is good to go. If not, Edwina can take care of it."

"Kane."

He stopped and glanced back at her, his expression completely masked, no vulnerability evident.

"Yes, Maggie?"

"Thanks."

"For what? The Penningtons are special to me. I should be thanking you for saving Ashley."

"For your help today." *For understanding and not pushing,* she finished silently.

He inclined his head toward her, then left. The door closing magnified the feeling of loneliness that had inundated Maggie earlier. She looked about at the chaos. She felt her life was like the items in the boxes, not one of them in its proper place.

Suddenly she needed to get away from the apartment. Walking into her bedroom, she dug through a box until she found her jogging clothes and her MP3 player. One of the best ways she had found to handle her stress was to exercise— hard. After donning her shorts, T-shirt and tennis shoes, she left to run until she was too exhausted even to think.

An hour later and bone tired, Maggie let herself into her apartment, removing her earplugs and placing her MP3 player on the table in the small foyer. The idea of a hot shower prodded her to move faster toward her bedroom even though her muscles ached from her grueling workout.

She entered the room, her gaze immediately fastening onto

the boxes stacked against one wall. An unfamiliar scent accosted her nostrils. The hairs on her nape tingled. She started to turn.

Thud!

Something hard slammed into the back of her head. As she crumbled to the floor, the blackness swallowed her up.

THREE

Pain pulsated a pounding rhythm against her skull. Maggie reached up and touched the spot that throbbed. A sticky substance coated her fingertips. Although the darkness reeled behind her closed eyes, she slowly opened the lids. Light assaulted her, and she shut them immediately.

What happened?

Again she inched her eyes open, letting them adjust to the brightness that illuminated her bedroom. She held her hand up in front of her face and saw the red that covered her skin.

Someone hit me?

She remembered coming into her apartment and heading for her bedroom. After that, a blank slate greeted her probing. She was lying prone on the hardwood floor so something had happened. But what?

As though in slow motion, she twisted to her side to push herself to her feet. Halfway up, the room spinning before her, she clutched the small table by the doorway to steady herself. It came crashing down on top of her. The books she had stacked on it tumbled into her and sent her collapsing to the floor. She hit her head in the same place that hurt. Pain streaked outward in waves that threatened to drive her back into the black void.

* * *

Edwina Bacon shuffled toward her recliner in front of her TV when she heard a loud noise as if something above her in Maggie's apartment struck the floor. After all that happened in the past month, the manager of Twin Oaks skirted her chair and made her way toward her front door. She jingled her keys in her pocket to make sure she had them and left her place.

With her hand on the ornate carved banister, she climbed the stairs as quickly as she could.

At Maggie's place, Edwina rang the bell.

Nothing.

She pressed in the white button a second time then a third.

With a glance from side to side, Edwina removed her key ring and found the one to Maggie's. If she wasn't home, what caused that sound? If she was home, why hadn't she answered the door?

Edwina inserted her key and paused before turning the handle. Memories of Henry's death only weeks before inundated her. She prayed this wasn't a repeat of what happened to Henry. For a few seconds she thought of going back down and calling Kane or her nephew at the police station.

Lord, what should I do?

What if Maggie had fallen and hurt herself and couldn't come to the door? What if she needed help *now?* With her teeth clenched, Edwina twisted the knob and pushed the door open.

"Maggie? Are you all right?"

Edwina stood in the entrance and glanced around. Relieved nothing seemed disturbed although there were still unopened boxes scattered about the living room, she moved a foot into the apartment, leaving the door wide open.

"Maggie," she called.

A moan sounded from the bedroom. Edwina hurried as fast as she could down the hallway. Her heart pounded with each step against the hardwood planks.

Then Edwina saw Maggie. She lay on the floor, her eyelids fluttering. Books were scattered about her, and a small table sat at an angle across her stomach.

With an effort, Edwina knelt next to Maggie. Edwina pressed her lips together to keep her own moan inside her at the pain in her aching knees. Maggie needed her help.

"Maggie," she touched the young woman's shoulder, "what happened?"

Maggie grimaced as her gaze connected with hers. "I'm not sure."

"Here, let me help you up." Edwina pushed the small table to the side, slid several books away and clasped the new tenant's arm.

She attempted to hoist herself up, but pain flitted across her features.

"Where are you hurt?" Edwina's gaze fixed on the red stain on the wooden floor.

Maggie sank back, drew in a deep breath and brought her hand to her head. "Here."

"Let me see." Gently Edwina turned the young woman's head and saw the gash and her hair matted with blood. "You must have hit your head hard when you fell."

"No."

The weakness of her denial made Edwina look back into Maggie's eyes, dulled with pain, the young woman's features pale with a gray tinge.

Silence reigned for a good minute, the new tenant's brow creased as though she were recalling something. "Someone hit me from behind."

"Someone was in here?"

"Yes," Maggie said in a more definitive voice. "When I came home from my jog, the person must have been in here waiting for me."

"Why?"

"I don't know. A robbery attempt?"

Edwina felt the shiver that shimmied down Maggie's body. "I'm calling my nephew. He's a detective with the police department. We can't have this in our apartment building. You lie right there while I get some help."

"But—"

"Don't move. I'll be right back." Edwina struggled to her feet, her breathing coming in gasps, and started for the door.

With her shock receding, a thought wormed its way into Maggie's mind. She could have been killed. Suddenly the idea of being by herself in her apartment caused her to blurt out, "Don't leave me."

Edwina halted. "Oh, dear me. I'm not leaving. I'm just going to make a few calls."

Maggie gestured toward the bedside table, finally managing to sit up slowly. "I've got a phone over there, and it's hooked up."

Edwina spotted it, and her face brightened into a smile. "That you do." She shuffled over to the bed and sat while she dialed.

Maggie listened to her make two calls, first to Kane then to her nephew David Morgan. Although Edwina's words were muffled, Maggie heard the concern in the older woman's voice. And Edwina's sober expression only confirmed the seriousness of Maggie's situation.

Maggie tried to think what she should do, but the throbbing pain encompassed her whole head now as though a marching band performed inside her skull. No coherent thoughts materialized, and she wilted back against the wall.

A few minutes later while Edwina was still talking to her nephew, someone entered her apartment. Hurried footsteps resonated down her hallway. Was her attacker returning to finish the job? Maggie tensed, that slight movement pulsating a warning to her brain she ignored. She labored to sit straight up, but the action increased the hammering pain in her head until she could no longer ignore her plight.

Kane appeared in her bedroom doorway. Exhaling her pent-up breath, Maggie wished she was anywhere but sprawled across the floor, her hair a tangled mess, her workout clothes askew. There was nothing dignified about her position, but she was so glad it wasn't the intruder returning.

"Edwina told me someone broke into your apartment."

Kane bent over and lifted her up into his arms as though she weighed ten pounds. As he walked to her bed, his clean scent of soap with a hint of pine wafted to her. She resisted the urge to lay her head on his shoulder and surrender to the blackness that edged closer with each jarring motion.

Gently, as though she was precious to him, Kane placed her on her coverlet. Its softness cocooned around her legs as she eased back against the headboard. She was careful not to get any blood on her linens, careful not to make any sudden moves or touch the place where her intruder struck her. "Thanks."

He hovered above her, the look on his face hard and somber. "You need to be checked out at the emergency room."

"I know." The pounding against her skull underscored her need to see a doctor. She knew the dangers of a concussion, and if the pain was any indication, she had a doozy.

Edwina hung up. "Kane, can you take Maggie to the hospital?"

"Yes."

Maggie wanted to protest but wouldn't. She hated being beholden to anyone, but she really didn't have much of a choice. She couldn't see driving herself to the emergency room.

Edwina turned toward Maggie. "I'm having David meet me here to check out your apartment. Then we'll come to the hospital. He'll get a statement from you there. Do you think anything is missing?"

So many of her things were still in boxes. Maggie, without moving her head, made a visual sweep of the room. "Nothing looks disturbed, but I'll need to go through what I have to be sure."

"I noticed your TV in the living room. Where's your jewelry? That's something else a burglar takes." Edwina pushed herself off the other side of the double bed.

"In the jewelry box on my dresser." Maggie pointed toward it.

Edwina retrieved it and set it in Maggie's lap. "You might want to check it."

She opened the intricately carved box of cherry wood that her father had given her two birthdays ago, right before he'd died. The thought pained her more than the ache in her head.

She didn't have much but the few valuable pieces—a gold cross on a delicate chain, a cameo pin, a ring with a large red garnet encircled with tiny diamonds and a pair of opal earrings— were all there among her costume jewelry. "Nothing's gone."

"Odd," Edwina muttered as she took the box back to the dresser.

Kane moved close. "Ready?"

Maggie inhaled a deep breath. "As ready as I'm going to be."

She started to swing her legs over the side of the bed at the same time Kane began to scoop her up into his arms. She held her hand up. "I can walk."

There was no way she wanted him to carry her to his car. The very thought sent panic through her. The twenty seconds she had been in his embrace earlier was all she cared to experience. *Liar*, she chided herself. She'd enjoyed the feel of his arms about her more than she wanted to admit.

But as she slowly rose from the bed, her wishes were

denied. The room rotated. She collapsed back and clutched the coverlet to keep herself upright. The jerking action, however, swirled the room faster. She closed her eyes, but that only caused the dark to revolve. Her stomach roiled. That was when Kane's strong arms enveloped her in their protective circle. Again he lifted her effortlessly and headed toward the door.

The exertion of holding her head up was too much for her. She surrendered to her earlier urge and laid her cheek against the cushion of his shoulder. The motion of him walking jounced her so she slid her eyes shut and bit down on her lower lip. Nausea continued to agitate her stomach. This bump on the noggin was worse than she'd thought.

"I don't want to stay overnight!" Maggie tried to keep her head steady because any movement sent pain through her and riled her stomach. When would the medication the doctor gave her start working?

Kane folded his arms across his chest. "Well, I'm not taking you home, and I doubt you're in any condition to walk the ten blocks."

"Did anyone tell you that you're not very accommodating?"

"Yep, many times."

The firm set of his mouth told her she wouldn't be able to budge him. Besides, he was right. She didn't think she could walk across the room without feeling sick. At least lying in this hospital bed kept the pain at a bearable level.

The door swished open, and Edwina, with a man in worn jeans and a sweatshirt, entered. A grin that dimpled Edwina's wrinkled cheeks appeared as she shuffled across the room.

"Maggie, I want you to meet my nephew, David Morgan. He's a detective with Seven Oaks Police Department and will be working your case."

The detective extended his hand, and Maggie shook it.

"It's nice to meet you. I just wish it were under different circumstances."

"Me, too. I took a look around your apartment. The intruder didn't disturb anything that Aunt Edwina and I could find, but I want you to go through it when you feel better and let me know for sure. Did you see anything?"

"No. Now that I've had time to think about it, I sensed something when I came into my bedroom and started to turn when I was hit from behind. I can't even tell you if it was a man or a woman."

David pulled out a pad with a stub for a pencil. "What did you sense?"

Maggie tried to remember what it was that alerted her to the fact something was different. A blank screen stretched before her. "I can't remember."

"Can you remember anything else?"

Maggie tried to replay the whole scene in her mind, but she always came up blank by the time she reached her bedroom. "No, everything seemed normal. My door was locked, and I let myself in. Nothing looked out of place."

"Are you sure it was locked?"

"Yes, why do you ask?"

"I couldn't find any signs of forced entry." David jotted something down on his pad.

"So how did the intruder get into her apartment?" Kane asked before Maggie had a chance.

"I don't know for sure. Could he have had a key? Maybe Henry gave one out to someone." David made another note.

"That doesn't sound like Henry, but I guess he could have," Edwina said, her lips pinched together.

"We may never know for sure. Maggie, let me know if you do remember anything else." Edwina's nephew dug into his back pocket and withdrew a card. "This is my number. Call me with anything you can remember, even if you think it's not important."

"Do you think this break-in has anything to do with the murder that occurred in the apartment?" Maggie voiced the question that had plagued her since she had awakened, especially since it was possible the intruder used a key that he somehow got from Henry.

David stroked his chin. "Maybe. I'm not sure what, though."

"Yeah, that's what has me puzzled." Maggie's gaze sought Kane. "Where are Henry's possessions? Who took them?"

"Edwina and I boxed them up, and they're in the basement. Henry doesn't have any relatives we can find."

"So there wasn't any reason for the murderer to break into my place."

Kane frowned. "Not that I can see, but I'm going to beef up the security. I'll be changing everyone's locks. I'm checking into getting a security system for the building."

"I'll be talking to your tenants to see if someone saw anything." David pocketed his pad and chewed pencil. "Aunt Edwina has already given me her statement. How about you, Kane? Did you hear or see something out of the ordinary?"

"No, since I came home earlier than I'd originally planned, I was in my workshop, finishing up a table. Until Edwina called, I didn't know anything had happened. I had my sander going and barely heard my cell phone ringing."

"I didn't see or hear anything, either, and when I went up the stairs, there was nobody around." Maggie shifted cautiously to make herself more comfortable—nothing helped.

Edwina took Maggie's hand and patted it. "Don't you worry. Tomorrow night at a building meeting in my apartment, I'll get everyone to be on the lookout. This won't happen again."

Maggie wished she could believe that. Although neighborhood watches were effective to a point, they didn't stop burglaries altogether. "Hopefully the robber saw that I didn't have much to steal and won't be back."

Edwina squeezed her hand. "I'm sure you're right, dear. The meeting will be at seven-thirty, and David's going to give a little talk about what we can do to be more alert."

Her nephew's eyebrows shot up. "I am?"

"Yes, I want the tenants to see the seriousness of the situation, and a detective's presence will make that point beautifully. Besides, I'm serving those cookies you love so much."

David grinned. "And tea?"

"Of course, dear. Decaf, however, since it's in the evening. I wouldn't want to be responsible for keeping anyone up all night." After another pat, Edwina released Maggie's hand. "We'll go and let you get some rest. This has been a trying day."

Trying day was putting it mildly. Maggie shifted again. But thankfully the pain's intensity had finally dulled slightly with the medication.

When Edwina and her nephew left, the energy in the room decreased to a normal level. "She's a ball of fire."

"I wouldn't be surprised if she started patrolling the halls," Kane said in a serious tone while a gleam danced in his eyes.

Maggie chuckled at that picture. "Don't make me laugh. It hurts too much."

Kane moved closer. "Seriously, Edwina's right. We'll need to be more alert. Too much has happened in my apartment building in the past month. I'll make what changes I can, but until the person who murdered Henry is caught, I won't feel safe."

"I agree. But it's been almost three weeks. The longer it goes unsolved the harder it will be."

"If you want to get out of your lease, I won't stop you."

"No!" Her fervent tone caused surprise to flare into his eyes. "I can't move again. Besides, I haven't got a connection to Henry, and there's nothing of value to steal, which I'm sure the thief discovered. My old TV wouldn't bring fifty dollars."

"Then we're going to have to hope the case is solved. The thing is Henry wasn't a well-liked man."

Maggie rubbed her temple. "Not liking a person doesn't mean you'd murder him."

"Let me put it another way. He was hated by a lot of people in Seven Oaks."

"Who?"

"Probably everyone who worked in his department and others at the university."

"Why?"

"He wasn't a nice man. He took pleasure in making life difficult for others."

Exhaustion cleaved to her. Maggie closed her eyes for a few seconds. "Are you one of those people?" When she peered at Kane again, she saw a glimpse of something that looked like distaste.

A shutter fell over his features. "He wasn't one of my favorite people."

The next evening Maggie entered Edwina's apartment ten minutes late for the building meeting. People crowded into the older woman's living room. In the short time Maggie had lived at Twin Oaks she had seen everyone at least once in the hallway, but she hadn't really gotten to know anyone except Edwina and Kane.

Especially not her birth mother. Besides yesterday when she'd helped Ashley, she'd only seen Vicky once today in the hallway. And that brief exchange had left her drained. She wasn't good at keeping secrets.

"How are you doing?" Edwina came forward to usher Maggie inside. "Let me introduce you to everyone." The older woman took her by the arm. "Now that Maggie has arrived, we can start our meeting. Since she's the new kid on the block, let's go around the room and introduce ourselves."

The person closest to Edwina tipped his head forward. "I'm Bradley Quinn. I don't live here, but my parents live upstairs right above you. They asked me to come and report back to them. Mom isn't feeling well, and Dad's at a high school function."

Maggie shook the tall, thin man's cold hand. His features should have been attractive except for the permanent frown lines about his mouth and on his forehead. His face, like his body, was long and thin with a mane of chestnut hair, shoulder length, that he kept fidgeting with.

"Bradley might as well live here. He spends a good deal of time with us. He's my nephew. I'll make sure I introduce you to my sister and her husband soon." Turning toward Bradley, Edwina grinned. "Tell Ann I'll make her some of my chicken soup. That ought to make her better in no time."

Maggie moved to the next person beside Bradley. A petite, dark-haired beauty that she knew to be Kyra Williams, Henry Payne's secretary. "I've seen you several times with a little boy."

"My son. Thankfully Edwina arranged for a high school student from our church to babysit the children at the Sellman's this evening while we meet."

"Normally Kenny watches them when we're nearby, but with all that has happened lately we thought it best to have an older teen." Edwina scrunched up her mouth. "I guess technically Kenny has eighteen months to go before he is an official teenager."

"Please don't remind us, Edwina."

The large, muscular man who had made that comment had to be John Pennington with blue eyes and a buzz cut. He sat next to Vicky, holding her hand.

"It's good to finally meet you since we live across the hall from each other." *And you're my mother's husband.* Maggie bit down on the inside of her mouth to keep those words quiet.

"You've met Vicky, John's wife." Edwina passed on to a couple next to Maggie's birth mother. "This is Thomas and Lisa Sellman. They live across the hall from me."

Maggie greeted both of them, trying to remember what Edwina had told her about Thomas and Lisa. He was a graduate student at Seven Oaks University, working part-time at the school while Lisa was a hairstylist. "It's nice to meet you two."

"Okay, now that the introductions have been made, let's get down to business." Edwina gestured for Maggie to take a seat on the couch next to Kane. "My nephew has been kind enough to come talk to us about what we can do to make this apartment safer for us and our families."

David Morgan rose from a rocking chair with his cup of tea in hand. He downed some then settled it back in its saucer on a small round table next to him. "Actually there are a lot of things you can do to make sure you all are as safe as possible. Being alert is paramount."

As David went into detail of how they could be more alert, Maggie scanned the people sitting around Edwina's living room. Her neighbors. All strangers. She was the outsider, something she was familiar with in her life. They all knew each other, from what Edwina had said, for a couple of years at the very least. Henry had been the last person to move into the building two years ago. Since that time, there hadn't been a vacancy until the murder.

The sense of being watched engulfed Maggie. She swept her gaze around the circle and found Vicky staring at her. Maggie tensed. Did she see something familiar? Panic took hold until the older woman smiled, her eyes crinkling with warmth. She nodded her head slightly then returned her attention to what David was saying. Maggie released a long sigh that didn't escape Kane's notice.

He leaned close. "You'll be safe. I'm making it my personal mission."

The intensity in his voice reassured her. At that moment she felt very safe.

After David finished speaking, Kane stood and moved forward. "Today all the doors to your apartments were checked to make sure they were solid wood and the hinges have non-removable pins. I changed the locks—adding dead bolts as well as peepholes so you can tell who has come to your door."

Kane's gaze snagged Maggie's. He had accomplished a lot in one day. Again the sense of security in his presence surprised her. She really didn't know him well, and yet she felt he would protect her at all costs.

"Now for the outside doors." Kane looked away from Maggie and made eye contact with each of his tenants. "I'm going to install a system where a person will have to buzz someone inside to be let into the building. It will be locked. People can go out but can't come in without someone letting them in or having a key."

"What about the children?" Vicky took a cookie from a plate that Edwina passed around the circle.

"I'll work with them. They'll get used to the system."

"I, for one, am elated that we'll have a system like you described. It makes me feel my son is safe. He could play in the hallway and I wouldn't worry about him." Kyra gave the cookie platter to Bradley, who was behind her wing chair.

"This will be better and will reassure Mom." Bradley reached around Kyra to hand the plate to John.

"David, are there any leads on who killed Henry?" John shifted his large frame on the love seat and rolled his shoulders as if he were stiff and sore.

"None to speak of."

"Was the break-in connected to the murder?" Lisa Sellman rose and walked to the teapot to pour herself some more.

"Yeah, was it connected?" Vicky's frown reminded Maggie of hers when she was really upset.

Tension flowed off her birth mother, affecting Maggie more than she cared to acknowledge. She didn't owe the woman anything.

"We don't know. With Kane's safety procedures and you all being more alert, there shouldn't be any more problems." David grabbed the last two cookies on the plate then placed it on the coffee table. "I have to get back to the station. You all know how to get in touch with me if you can think of anything from the day Henry was killed or yesterday when Miss Ridgeway's apartment was broken into." He strode toward the door.

Edwina hurried after her nephew. "Thanks for coming. See you at church on Sunday."

David kissed his aunt on the cheek and left. The click of the door as he closed it sounded in the quiet. No one said anything for a good minute. John chewed his cookie. Lisa drank her tea. Kyra stared a hole into the carpet at her feet.

The anxiety, created by Vicky's presence, in Maggie increased until she felt as if she would snap in two pieces. She couldn't shake the idea that the break-in and the murder were connected, although she wasn't sure why.

Suddenly a thought gripped her. *Has anyone checked Henry's possessions lately to see if they have been disturbed?*

Maggie clasped Kane's arm. His gaze swung to her. "After the meeting, can we check Henry's things in the basement?"

"You think someone's gone through them?"

"I don't know. Maybe."

"Then let's do it now." Kane came to his feet and offered Maggie his hand.

For a few seconds she stared at it, his fingers long and strong from gripping a sanding block. He created beautiful pieces of furniture with those hands. She fit hers within his and allowed him to help her stand. Her vision wavered from the quick movement. She wasn't used to taking it slow and easy. With him close, she ambled toward the small foyer in Edwina's apartment.

"You two leaving?" Edwina asked, cutting off their escape.

"Yes, it's been a long day, and I'm still not feeling one hundred percent." All of which was true, but Maggie didn't want to say anything to anyone about where she and Kane were going before she returned to her own apartment. No sense alarming the tenants anymore than they already were. Besides it was probably nothing. Just her trying to make some sense out of something random.

"Dear, I don't want you to worry about breakfast. I'm bringing you some tomorrow morning."

"You don't have—"

"Of course, I don't have to. I want to." Edwina's two dimples appeared in her wrinkled cheeks. "Call me in the morning when you get up. I'll bring it then."

Kane reached around Maggie to open the door. His arm brushed up against hers, his touch jolting her. She took a small step back.

Edwina grasped her hand and squeezed it. "Will you be okay upstairs by yourself in your apartment?"

"Sure," Maggie said without thinking. On second thought, she wasn't so positive about her answer. She'd spent the night in the hospital and had only stayed in her apartment a few hours before coming to Edwina's. In that time she'd checked the new locks on her door several times and had jumped at any sound she'd heard.

"I have a spare bedroom for guests. You can stay with me if you want."

While Kane moved out into the hall, Maggie turned toward Edwina and hugged her. "Edwina, you're so kind to offer. I may not have been here long, but that apartment is my home now. I won't let anyone run me off. I'll deal with it. God is with me."

Edwina's eyes twinkled. "That He is. Are you still coming with me to church on Sunday?"

"I wouldn't miss it for the world. I should be fine by then. Good night, Edwina, and again thanks for the offer."

Maggie stared back at the door as the older woman closed it. Edwina was wonderful and kind. She'd been lucky to find someone like her in Seven Oaks, in the very building she lived in. She felt so alone here without any family and friends. And now with Vicky across the hall, seeing her every day but not being a part of her life, the loneliness was even more evident.

"Ready?" Kane headed toward the back of the house and the steps that led to the basement.

"I'm not sure if I want to find something missing or not." Maggie followed him down the stairs.

"We'll know shortly and deal with it either way." Kane unlocked the door to the large storage area and let Maggie enter first.

The huge room was partitioned into cages where the tenants could store their belongings they didn't need in their apartments. Kane crossed to the far wall to the cage next to hers.

"This is an extra one I have in case someone needs more space." He searched for the key to the cage, and when he found it on his ring, he reached for the padlock.

After unlocking the chain link entrance, Kane advanced inside. Maggie came up beside him. With a deep scowl, he swung around and stared at the padlock then back at the stacked boxes.

"What's wrong?" Apprehension washed over Maggie as though she had been caught in a sudden downpour.

"Someone has been in here."

FOUR

"How can you tell?" Maggie scanned the boxes in the cage in the storeroom and didn't see anything that looked out of place. Everything was neat, piled around the perimeter in orderly rows two deep.

Kane pointed to three of the boxes that were in back with four on each side of them. "Because I stacked the back row four high and the second one three exactly. One's missing."

"Are you sure?" The implication meant the intruder probably had been after something he'd thought was in the apartment.

"Yes." His jaw hardened into a firm line.

She gestured to his key ring. "Is that the only key to the padlock?"

"Edwina has the other one."

"Would she have a reason to take one of Henry Payne's boxes?"

"No, and they were heavy. She can't lift anything over ten pounds. I can't see her taking a box for any reason."

"Then that means someone picked the padlock."

"Or took Edwina's key."

The damp chill in the cage seeped into her bones. "Who has a key to this room?"

"Only the tenants in the building." Kane walked to the

storeroom's entrance and checked the lock. "This looks okay."

Not liking the idea that one of the tenants took Henry's possessions, Maggie moved to the cage's padlock. She bent down and examined it. "Has this always had scratch marks on it?"

Kane inspected it, too. "No. It's brand-new. I didn't have a padlock for this cage until I needed it for Henry's possessions."

"Picking a lock isn't easy. Maybe it was a burglar who knew what he was doing." She hoped that was the case and not something tied to the murder and the people at Twin Oaks Apartments.

"Then how did he get in here?"

She shrugged. "With a key, or he picked that lock, too, and it doesn't show."

"I'm glad I'm getting added security on the doors into the building."

But that wouldn't help if the culprit was someone in the building. The very idea chilled her. "Someone probably read about the murder and saw an opportunity to steal from a dead man. You know how some robbers read the obits and see when a person's funeral is then go rob him when everyone is at the service." She wanted to believe that, but in her heart she knew that wasn't the answer. Maybe Henry had something valuable one of the tenants decided to steal.

"I suppose that could be the case, but…"

"That might also explain why the burglar came to my apartment. Maybe he didn't know I'd moved in. I've only been here a short time. You hadn't advertised in the paper about renting the apartment yet."

"Yeah, but his funeral was weeks ago, so the thief certainly took his time. And I didn't put these boxes in here until the police were through."

"The police didn't release the apartment until recently." *Am*

I grasping at straws? Trying to convince myself it isn't a neighbor? Maggie hooked her hair behind her ears.

"I guess it's a possibility…" Frowning, Kane shoved his hand through his hair. "Since Henry didn't have any close relatives or friends for that matter, who's to know what's missing exactly."

"That's sad that he didn't have anyone." Maggie leaned against the wall, her exhaustion catching up with her.

"You didn't know Henry. I don't feel sorry for him."

The brief flash of anger that descended over Kane's features took Maggie by surprise. He didn't usually show his emotions like that. What had Henry done to him to cause those kinds of feelings? "Then why did you rent to him?"

"Because being mean isn't a good enough reason to evict a person who paid his rent on time and didn't disturb the neighbors with loud music. He was a good tenant. My hands were tied."

Were they? Or was there more to it? Maggie shook the nagging questions from her mind. She didn't like the direction her thoughts were taking her. She was beginning to suspect everyone around her, and she had no real reason to do that. She hadn't known Henry, and his murder wasn't her problem. She had enough of her own to deal with—namely, what was she going to do about Vicky Pennington?

"This almost seems futile. I'll have to look into a better lock for this door and each cage."

"And maybe you and Edwina should be the only ones with a key to the storeroom." His eyebrows rose, and she quickly added, "At least until everything is solved concerning Henry."

"So you're thinking what I've been thinking and not wanting to voice aloud?"

Their gazes connected, and a bond instantly leaped between them. "Yep. It could be a tenant."

"I hope we're wrong." Kane closed the door and secured it. "I'll walk you to your apartment." A shutter fell over his features as if he were closing down his emotions.

"You don't have to. I think I can find my way to my place." Maggie sent him a grin, wanting to lighten the mood after their discovery of the theft and its ramifications.

"With all that's happened, humor me." The grim lines of his mouth indicated the opposite of humor.

Maggie went first up the narrow steps to the main level, conscious of Kane behind her. The hairs on her nape tingled. Uncomfortable with his intense gaze, she made it a point to be next to him on the wider staircase to the second floor.

At her door, she turned toward Kane to thank him. That intensity in his expression wiped the words from her mind.

Finally he blinked and shook his head. "Sorry. I'm still trying to get past the theft and that it could be someone I know. I realize Henry had some valuable things, but why just one box?"

"Good question. Are you going to call David Morgan?"

"Yes. Although it probably has nothing to do with Henry's murder, David needs to know there was a robbery even if we can't figure out what was taken."

"Well, thank you for walking me to my apartment." She twisted around to unlock her door. As she stepped into her place, memories of her attacker swamped her and she hesitated, the dull ache in her head a constant reminder of what happened the day before.

"Are you all right?"

"Just tired." She wasn't ready to admit her reluctance to come back to the apartment after the intrusion. This was her home now, and yet she felt violated, the feeling of security elusive.

"Would you humor me some more? I'd like to check out your place before I leave."

Was it that obvious what was going on in her? She glanced

at the mirror she'd hung in the hall, and all she saw were weary lines and dark circles under her eyes caused by her recent ordeal. "You don't have to."

"I know, but when someone intruded into your apartment, I feel as if he also broke into mine. I'd do the same for anyone in this building."

The last sentence was added after a ten second pause as though he needed her to know it was only business. She got the message loud and clear, but that didn't stop the disappointment from surging. She tamped it down. She had no business even looking at a man at the moment, let alone considering anything else.

Maggie waited by the door while Kane first checked the two bedrooms, then the living room and kitchen. Ten minutes later he stood in front of her again.

"All clear. Here's my card. If you hear or see anything suspicious, call me. I can be here in less than a minute." He laid the card in her palm.

The touch of his fingers focused all her senses on him. A light woodsy scent drew her toward him while the warmth and concern in his gaze telegraphed the danger in this attraction. He'd made it plain he was a loner, like her. She needed to respect his wishes and yet—

She pulled back. "Thanks for looking around. I know your new security measures will help, but it…" She didn't know how to put into words her feelings of anger and sadness that at odd times during the past twenty-four hours had produced a lump in her throat.

"But you lost a certain amount of innocence yesterday."

She tilted her head. "You're right. I hadn't thought of it that way. Until someone breaks into your home, you don't think it will happen to you. That only happens to the other guy, not you."

"Even with the university, the crime rate in Seven Oaks

isn't high. Then in less than a month two crimes have happened in my building. That doesn't sit well with me." His own anger threaded through his words and carved frown lines into his face.

"Do you have an inventory of Henry's boxes? Maybe if we figure out what was taken, that might help Edwina's nephew."

"Edwina boxed up his belongings, but she didn't make an inventory that I know of."

"I'll ask her tomorrow when she comes for breakfast." Maggie moved to the door, grasped the knob and leaned into the wooden edge, all the activity catching up with her. Fatigue weighed her down. "Would you mind if Edwina and I went through the boxes left if she doesn't have an inventory? Maybe she'll be able to figure out what's missing."

"No, I don't mind. There isn't anyone to claim Henry's possessions. I'm going to keep them for a while just in case someone comes forward that we don't know about. But why the interest?"

Maggie lifted her shoulders in a shrug. "Oh, I don't know. I can't shake the feeling everything is connected."

"What makes you think that?"

"For the very reason not many crimes happen around here and suddenly several do in a short space of time." Despite her protests that she didn't need to get involved, here she was getting involved. But she wouldn't sleep well until Henry's murderer was caught. "Also someone probably used a key to get into my apartment and the storeroom. How did the intruder get ahold of not just one but two keys? Seems like a lot of trouble for just a plain ole burglary. There are easier targets than that."

Kane smiled. "You've got a point. Are you going to give David a run for his money?"

"No way. I just don't want anyone visiting me again."

"They won't if I can help it."

The fervent tone in his voice reassured Maggie, but then some things were out of their control. She knew that firsthand. "I appreciate what you've done. Thanks."

Kane went out into the hallway and turned back toward her. "You're welcome. Call, if you need me."

When Maggie shut the door, she collapsed against it and stared into her living room. *Call, if you need me.* Those words rang through her mind. There was something about Kane McDowell that tempted her to discover more about the man.

"Not good, Maggie," she muttered to herself as she pushed away from the door, mentally doing the same with thoughts of Kane, and ambled toward her bedroom.

She paused in the doorway and scanned the area, her attention finally resting on the spot on the floor where she'd fallen. Memories of the day before again deluged her as though a storm rampaged through her. Was the intruder yesterday tied to the murder or a robber looking for valuables? At the moment she didn't even know which one she wanted it to be. If the break-in was tied to the murder, the person would have no reason to come back now that he knew someone else lived in Henry's apartment. If he'd been looking for something, it probably was in the box taken from the storeroom. If it was a burglar, with the new security measures that should be all that was needed to keep her safe. She should be all right either way. But if it was someone in the apartment building, what did that do to her theory?

Even though Kane had checked out the room, she knelt and looked under the bed. Dust bunnies were all that greeted her inspection. She rose and started for the closet. Out of the corner of her eye she saw her Bible on the table next to her bed. Her fear and earlier thought about things not being in a person's control made her seek guidance from the One who did control life.

In Job 11, Maggie found what she needed to sleep. In the Lord's hands she would be safe. *And thou shalt be secure, because there is hope; yea, thou shalt dig about thee, and thou shalt take thy rest in safety.*

"This is delicious, Edwina. You can fix me breakfast anytime." Maggie popped the last bite of the lemon poppy seed muffin into her mouth. She'd probably have to exercise every day next week just to work off the calories from the two large ones she'd devoured. Then again she hadn't eaten much yesterday, so maybe it would all balance out.

"Are you sure you don't want some of my tea? It comes from England."

"No. My body is used to at least four or five cups of coffee before noon. I think it would go into shock if I fed it anything else."

"Talk about going into shock. I can't believe someone took one of Henry's boxes." Edwina pushed herself to her feet and shuffled over to the coffeepot on the counter. She brought it to the table and poured some into Maggie's mug.

"Please, you don't have to wait on me."

Edwina smiled. "This is my treat even if we're in your kitchen."

Maggie doctored her brew with milk and one scoop of sugar. "Do you think you and I could go through Henry's boxes in the basement? If you can figure out what's missing, maybe we can come up with a reason why someone would take that box out of all the ones there."

The older woman's eyes sparkled with a lively gleam. "We could be detectives. I love reading mysteries, and it would be interesting to try some of the techniques I've learned over the years of reading them." She leaned across the table. "Personally, I think that's where David got his love for police work."

"From you?"

Edwina nodded. "He spent time with me in the summers when his parents went on vacation. I always had a mystery lying around. When he was older, he started reading them, too."

"When do you have some time?"

"Let's do it tomorrow after church."

"You've got yourself a date."

"Speaking of dates, are you going out with anyone?"

Maggie caught her breath in surprise. She stared at the mischievous look in Edwina's eyes. "I—I—no."

"Kane's been alone too long."

"You aren't very subtle."

"No one has ever accused me of being subtle."

Maggie chuckled. "That's one of the things I like about you, but don't get it in your head to try and fix me and Kane up. I'm not interested."

Edwina tapped her finger against her chin. "Let me see. You sat next to him on my couch last night. You left with him, and you say you aren't interested?"

Maggie rested her elbow on the table and cupped her chin in her palm. "Have you ever noticed how vulnerable he is?"

Edwina's soft laughter permeated the kitchen. "Kane vulnerable? I never thought to describe him as that, but—" she peered off into space for a moment "—now that I think about it, you're right. How perceptive you are. He didn't used to be like that. The war changed him. He'd just gotten engaged to Ruth when his Army Reserve unit was called up and he had to go to Iraq. When he came back from recuperating at his parents' in Florida from an injury that cut short his tour of duty, all he said about Ruth leaving Seven Oaks was she had a better offer in Dallas. He never talked about her after that."

"He never said why they weren't getting married?"

"Nope. In fact, he said little to anyone. He retreated to his basement workshop. He fixed up an apartment across the hall from it so he could live down there. He used to live in the Sellmans' apartment."

"So no one knows why his engagement was broken off?" Maggie took a sip of her coffee.

"That's between Kane and Ruth."

"What kind of injury did he sustain?"

Edwina shrugged. "He doesn't talk about it with anyone." She paused and tapped her chin. "Come to think of it when John moved in a few months later, I got the impression that they talked about it, but then that wouldn't be so unusual since John served with him."

Her curiosity aroused, Maggie wanted to pump Edwina for more information, but then she didn't want her to think she was interested in Kane. If her landlady thought that, she would never have any peace.

Ha! By the gleam in Edwina's eyes, she already thought it, so Maggie better prepare herself for more attempts.

"When I asked about his move to the basement once, he told me it was closer to his workshop and easier for him. He's been thinking of making furniture full-time lately. Demand for his pieces has grown quite a bit in the last year."

"Quit working at the university?"

"Yeah, he doesn't need the job. When his great-aunt died and left him with this house years ago, she also left him with a sizable inheritance, part of which he used to convert the mansion into an apartment building."

Maggie bit back another question concerning Kane. She didn't need to encourage the woman any more than she already had. Instead, she asked, "Do you have any kind of list of Henry's possessions?"

"Not in so many words." Edwina touched her temple. "It's

all stored up here. I may be seventy, but my mind is sharp as any twenty-year-old's."

"So you—" The sound of the doorbell interrupted Maggie's reply. "Who could that be?"

"There's only one way to find out. Go answer it."

Maggie hurried into the foyer, aware that Edwina had followed. When Maggie opened the door, Vicky Pennington had started back toward her apartment. The sight of her birth mother whisked any words of greeting from Maggie's mind. She stared at the woman's retreating figure.

Glancing over her shoulder when Edwina cleared her throat, Vicky saw Maggie and came back toward her with a plate in her hand. "I didn't think you were home. Hi, Edwina. I know you brought Maggie something for breakfast, but I thought since I made several cheesecakes this morning, you might like one, Maggie. I haven't gotten a chance to formerly welcome you to the building and give you a housewarming gift."

Edwina squeezed past Maggie. "Take it. Vicky's cheesecake is the best." The older woman walked toward the staircase.

Seconds evolved into half a minute before Maggie managed to lick her dry lips. "Mmm. Thanks. I love cheesecake. Come on in, and I'll cut us a piece." The thud of her rapid heartbeat thundered in her ears.

Vicky glanced back at her closed door. "I can't stay long, but after this week, I deserve a piece, even if it's mid-morning."

Her thinking exactly. When she was upset, Maggie ate sugar-laden food. A bad habit she wished she could break. At least she jogged to help keep her weight down. "A bad week?" Maggie walked into the kitchen and began making a fresh pot of coffee, glad to do something to keep her quivering hands busy.

"Being the secretary to the university president, I had to work overtime several nights because of the school's centennial celebration in a few weeks. I hate doing that. I have so little time with Kenny and Ashley as it is. And then of course, that scare with Ashley. No matter what you tell your kids about staying home alone, it doesn't look like you can prepare them for every kind of emergency that might arise. I never thought one of my children would choke on some food."

I can't do this! Panic attacked Maggie's nerves, renting them to shreds. "Your son's quite a young man." Maggie steadied her hand as she tried to cut two pieces of the cheesecake.

"That he is. But if Edwina didn't live nearby, I think I'd go crazy worrying about the kids every afternoon after school."

Did you worry about me? Do you ever think about the daughter you gave up? Why did you do it? Question after question bombarded Maggie, demanding answers. Finally alone with the woman, she drew in one deep breath then another before she pivoted to face her birth mother. Maggie placed the plates on the table and sat across from Vicky as though nothing were wrong, that her insides weren't wavering from the woman's presence.

Vicky looked about the kitchen. "This was the first room I put in order when we moved in. A home can't function without a kitchen. I certainly don't envy your job of putting everything away. I've lived here over three years and hope never to move again."

"Have you always lived in Seven Oaks?"

"No, but I grew up here. Where did you live before this?"

"St. Louis."

"Even with a population of seventy thousand, Seven Oaks is small compared to St. Louis."

"Easier to get around in. St. Louis was a little too big for me."

"That's the way I felt about the places I lived."

No, I don't want us to have any similarities. Maggie took a bite of her cheesecake, forcing it down her tight throat. "Edwina's right. This is delicious."

"It's an old family recipe. My mother was quite a cook and passed down a lot of recipes to me before she died."

As though she'd been punched in her stomach, Maggie's muscles knotted, pain radiating outward. She kept her gaze on the cheesecake and tried to school her features into a neutral expression, but Kane was so much better at it than she was.

"Do you like to cook?" Vicky brushed her short brown hair behind her ears.

Maggie picked at her dessert, wishing she could get a handle on her reeling emotions, as if she'd ridden the Tilt-a-Whirl at the state fair. "I get by." She slowly lifted her gaze to Vicky's. "That's about all I can say about my cooking skills. My mom didn't care much for the kitchen. I guess I'm the same way." Her thoughts spun from the confused tangle of her feelings, not one taking hold for even a few seconds.

God expected her to forgive Vicky for giving her up for adoption, but she didn't know if she could. She'd spent lonely years in foster homes, waiting for a couple to want her enough to adopt her. She'd spent the rest of her childhood trying to please a woman who hadn't really wanted any children. She thanked the Lord every day for her dad, but now even he was gone from her life.

"You don't sound convinced?" Vicky asked.

"I never took the time to learn to cook beyond reading the directions on the backs of microwave dinners. First school then my work demanded so much of my time."

"I teach a four-week cooking class starting next Wednesday night at the high school. It's from eight to ten. I don't usually recruit my students, but in this case I hope you'll join us. We have a lot of fun. I pick a nationality and center the sessions on that country. The first week's lesson is about Italian food. My mother was Italian. I think that's where I got my love for cooking."

*How in the world did I ever think I could calmly sit across
from her and talk as if we're friends? Lord, help me to make
it to the end of this conversation without shouting the truth at
this woman.*

Maggie rose and poured two cups of coffee. One part of
her wanted to grab at anything the woman had to offer, to learn
everything there was about Victoria Pennington. The other
part felt guilty as if she were betraying her adoptive parents—
especially her adoptive mother who hadn't returned any of her
calls in months since she'd discovered what she had been
doing—for even sitting here and listening to Vicky.

"I don't know," Maggie finally said as she sat down. "My
schedule is so chaotic right now."

"The class doesn't start for a few days. Just let me know
if you want to come, and I'll take care of the rest. It's the least
I can do after what you did for Ashley."

Maggie waved her hand. "That was nothing. I'm just glad
I was here to help."

Vicky frowned. "So am I." After taking a long sip of her
coffee, she looked Maggie straight in the eye. "Do you think
you could show Kenny the Heimlich maneuver?"

"Of course, I will," Maggie answered quickly, eager for any
time she could spend with her half brother.

"Oh, good," Vicky said with a sigh. "I'll feel much better
if he knows. I pray that never happens again, but it doesn't
hurt to cover every base." After finishing her piece of
cheesecake and taking a few more sips of coffee, she stood.
"I'd better get back to the trenches. Saturday morning is
cleanup day, and if I'm not there to supervise, nothing is
ever done."

"Yeah, I have a few boxes to unpack." Maggie trailed the
older woman to the small foyer. She needed to be alone.

At the door, Vicky said, "By the way, I wanted to invite you to dinner tomorrow night. It's our family night. It's when I go all out. Can you come?"

Family night! The tightness in Maggie's chest threatened her breathing. She nodded, unable to say a word.

"Good. Dinner's at seven. Come a little early. I think Kenny wants to show you something."

When Maggie was left alone in her apartment, she leaned into the hall table, gripping its edges, her eyes sliding closed. Quiver after quiver rippled down her length. *A special family dinner every Sunday night. Grew up in Seven Oaks. Italian heritage.* Fragmented thoughts bombarded her. She pressed her hands into her eyes and wished she could clear her mind. Everything was happening too fast as if she were falling into a bottomless pit. She didn't have any time to take it in and digest the information slowly.

But if she could manage to approach the situation unemotionally, she couldn't help thinking dinner Sunday night would be the perfect place to start getting some of her answers, so she could leave and return to her normal life.

FIVE

"This one is the last box," Maggie said as she brought it to Edwina, who was perched on a chair that Kane had moved into the storeroom.

The older woman opened the container, inspected its contents and picked up part of a coffeemaker. "Henry hated coffee. I could never understand why he kept this out on his countertop."

"For people who visited?"

Edwina laughed. "He wasn't one to offer a person something to drink unless he wanted it, too." Shaking her head, she continued, "Besides, he didn't have too many people visiting. If they came, they didn't stay long. He was a strange man."

"He sounds awful. Surely he had some redeeming qualities."

The older woman placed the coffeemaker back in the box and closed the lid. "Yes, believe it or not, he gave a lot of money to a rec center for underprivileged children in Seven Oaks."

"Why? That doesn't sound like the man I've been hearing about."

"I don't know why. He didn't share much of himself with anyone." Edwina taped the container up.

Just like Kane, Maggie thought and scanned the already checked boxes. "Do you know what's missing?"

"Yep, Henry's laptop and other desk items."

"Did he have a desktop computer, too?"

"No, only the laptop at home, and I know that my nephew checked it before releasing it."

Maggie sat on a box. "I wonder what was on it."

"I can call David and find out, but computers are easy to pawn."

"Yes, but what about Henry's stamp collection? It wasn't touched and my dad had one. He had several stamps worth a lot of money."

Edwina snapped her fingers. "I recall Henry bragging about a one of a kind he'd finally tracked down and purchased."

"Okay, then it could be someone searching for something in Henry's possessions—possibly on his computer."

"But how many people realize how valuable a stamp collection can be?"

"Maybe the person didn't have time to check all the boxes."

"Or he found exactly what he was looking for." Edwina rubbed her hand into the small of her back.

"What were the other items in the box besides the laptop?"

"Mostly papers, a few things he had in his drawer like a photo of a young girl, some pens and pencils..." Edwina tapped her chin and stared at the far corner for a moment before adding, "and items like paper clips and rubber bands. The usual things in a desk drawer. Again obviously nothing my nephew thought would be a motive for murder."

"A photo of a young girl? Did you recognize her?"

Edwina shrugged. "No. Maybe a lost love although it looked more current than that."

Was the photo a clue? Maggie shook her head. *Probably not because if so the intruder would have only taken it.*

"Did you figure out what was missing?" Kane asked from the doorway.

Maggie's heartbeat sped up at the sound of his voice. When she glanced at him, he was leaning against the doorjamb, his arms crossed over his chest, warmth in his gaze. "Henry's laptop and a few items from the desk."

"My, I'm ready for a nap." Edwina shoved to her feet. "I'll give David a call and let him know what's gone and see if he'll tell me anything about what they found on the computer."

"I imagine if they had found something, they would have kept it for evidence." Kane stepped into the room while Edwina passed him.

"You're probably right," Edwina said as she scurried down the hall.

"She sure moves fast for someone who's tired enough for a nap." Maggie chuckled and started to lift the box.

Kane beat her to it, his hands brushing hers away. "I'll take care of this."

She straightened and backed up a few paces toward the door while he effortlessly stacked the container on top of the pile. Edwina's matchmaking attempt the day before paraded across her mind. *What happened between Kane and his fiancée? What happened in the war to change him so much? And why am I focusing on him and not the reason I'm here?*

"I'd hoped to be able to help you all, but I received a call from the president of the university."

"Is there something wrong?"

"There's been another negative article in the newspaper in Lexington about the murder, on the first page no less. He's concerned about how this will affect enrollment."

"I imagine those types of headlines wouldn't be too good for a university."

"Especially when the killer is still at large." Kane locked the cage, gesturing toward the boxes inside it. "So what do you think? Is the break-in connected to Henry's murder?"

"Maybe, but it's hard to tell. Either way I should be all right because of the extra precautions you've put in place. Plus, the attacker now knows I live in the apartment. I certainly don't have much worth stealing." Maggie exited the storage room, pausing in the hallway while Kane locked the door and pocketed the key ring.

"Although I agree you should be safe, I'm not going to rest well until the murderer is caught." Kane stopped in front of the entrance into his apartment. "I understand from Edwina you're going to the Penningtons' tonight for dinner."

"Does the whole building know?"

"Pretty much. Although I'm not sure if Kyra has returned from her weekend trip." Silent laughter brightened his eyes.

"What Edwina knows obviously doesn't stay with her."

"Nope." He turned toward his door. "I'll see you tonight," he added and slipped inside his apartment before Maggie could ask what he meant by that. Was he going to be at the Penningtons', too?

The very thought made her steps light as she headed up the stairs. Maybe it wouldn't be so bad if he were there.

At her apartment door two hours later Maggie stopped, her hand on the knob. This was worse than the first time she had gotten up in front of a large audience in high school and given a campaign speech. Her heart fluttered like a flag in a brisk wind. After wiping her damp palms on her jeans, she touched her cameo, drawing silent support from the knowledge of her adoptive father's love. Between his love and the Lord's, she knew she could do anything.

Determinedly she crossed the hall to the Penningtons'. The door opened a second after her knock.

Kenny's grin looked like a big half moon. "You came!" He stepped aside for her to enter. "We're having lasagna!"

"I get the feeling you like lasagna." His enthusiasm was contagious, and Maggie matched his smile with her own.

"Yep. Mom's is the best."

Before Maggie was halfway into the living room, another rap echoed through the place. When Kenny opened the door to reveal Kane standing in the hallway, the warmth she felt at her brother's greeting evolved into an all-encompassing awareness of the man at the door.

"Uncle Kane!" Ashley ran into the living room and threw her arms around him. "Come." She tugged on his hand, leading him off in the direction of the bedrooms.

He threw a helpless look over his shoulder. "Be back in a sec."

"Ashley's showing Uncle Kane our new pet. I'm the one who gets to keep the snake for my science class for the month." Kenny's chest puffed out, his expression proud. "Wanna see?"

"Sure." *I think*, she added silently, not really sure if she should be in the same room with Kane any more than necessary. He was totally undermining her resolve to heed his advice and not get involved with him.

When Maggie stepped into Kenny's bedroom, she saw Ashley, with a big grin on her face, hand the snake to Kane. The little girl glanced at Maggie, dropped her gaze to the floor and scooted around behind Kane. When she stuck her thumb in her mouth, Maggie fought her impulse to hug the child to her. Every time she saw Ashley with her thumb in her mouth, Maggie thought of herself at the age of five at the foster home, sucking her thumb, scared of so many things in the world around her, desperately wanting a family who loved her and would keep her.

"Would you like to hold it?" Kane asked, a gleam dancing in his eyes as he held the reptile out for Maggie to take.

From his smug expression, Maggie was sure Kane thought

her worried look was because of the snake. She took the animal from him and stretched her arm out, allowing the reptile to slide up it.

The look of astonishment on Kane's face caused her to laugh. "When I was growing up, I had a snake. I think I was the only girl in the school who did."

"You did?" Kenny's eyes widened. "Mom wasn't gonna let me keep him at first. Dad talked her into it. Mom's scared of them."

"So was I at first. But I discovered the best way to get over a fear is to confront it head-on." As the garter snake curled around her arm, Maggie glanced up at Kane. He stared at her with a strange, though unreadable, expression on his face.

"Tell that to Mom. I think she would die if Rosie ever got loose in the apartment."

With her gaze still bound to Kane's, Maggie asked, "Ashley, would you like to put the snake back in its cage?" When the child didn't say anything, Maggie peered down at her sister, who still stood partially hidden behind Kane. The girl's brow was furrowed in a deep frown, her gaze riveted to the floor.

"I'll take him. Ashley doesn't talk much around new people." Kenny put the reptile back in its aquarium.

She didn't want to be a stranger to her own sister. A sudden surge of anger gripped Maggie, the walls of the bedroom closing in on her.

"Kenny. Ashley. I need your help," Vicky called from the end of the hallway.

At the door, Kenny spun around. "Uncle Kane, remember you're supposed to help us with the—" he glanced at Maggie "—dessert."

"Yeah, be right there."

As Kenny and Ashley left the bedroom, Maggie avoided Kane's probing gaze, turning her back on him as though she were fascinated with the children's exit. She needed her emotional strength for the next few hours. She couldn't afford the luxury of giving in to her newfound feelings concerning Kane. She concentrated, instead, on the feelings of abandonment and anger that she experienced standing in the middle of her siblings' bedroom, unable to say anything about who she was to them and wanting desperately to be a part of their lives as a sister would be.

When she had planned her move to Seven Oaks in the safe emotional comforts of St. Louis, she hadn't thought she would feel this kind of anger at her birth mother. She'd only wanted answers about her biological family.

Kane's hand settled on her shoulders. "What's wrong?"

Maggie wanted to lean back against him just for a few precious moments of comfort. Strangely she knew he would give her the solace she needed if she dared to ask. But that would be all. Kane McDowell wasn't looking for anything else in his life. If anything, he was running away from something that he wasn't ready to discuss with anyone. She had enough problems facing her; she couldn't take on his.

She shook her head, blinking away the tears that lately were so close to the surface. "It's nothing."

"I don't buy that. I'm a good listener, Maggie, but I learned long ago not to force someone to talk until they're ready." Kane's hands kneaded the stiff cords of her shoulders. "I won't let anything happen to you while you live here. We'll figure out what's going on."

She let him assume it was about the break-in. He hadn't known her long, and he was protective of her because he felt responsible for what was happening at Twin Oaks. Slowly the tension slipped from her body. Relishing the feel of his fingers on her, she wished she could talk about Vicky Pennington with him; but he had a bond with the family that went beyond friendship. Besides, it wasn't really her secret to reveal. Vicky had started her secrecy twenty-eight years ago, and it would be Vicky's place to end it.

"You know, Kane, I'm a good listener, too."

The motion of his hands ceased, his tautness conveyed in the tightening of his fingers on her shoulders. Even though her back was to him, she felt him distancing himself from her as if invisible lines, transmitting his feelings to her, connected them.

"I'm here if you need me," she heard herself say in the stark stillness of the room. Was it his fiancée leaving him or something else?

He leaned close to her ear. "Thanks, Maggie. That's the nicest thing anyone has said to me in a long time."

His whispered words caressed her heart. When he turned her around and tilted her chin so she could look him in the eye, she could hardly support herself. His gaze robbed her of any rational response.

"Uncle Kane! C'mon," Kenny shouted from the hallway.

Kane sighed. "Why don't you go into the living room, Maggie? This shouldn't take too long—I hope."

Thankful for Kenny's timely interruption, she hurried into the living room and sat, her back straight, her hands folded in her lap, as if any second she were going to break. Every time she was in Kane's presence she found herself drawn more and more to him against her better judgment. Where was her self-control when she needed it?

John Pennington appeared in the doorway from the kitchen. "I've been sent in here to keep you company. No one's allowed a moment of peace in this apartment." He sat across from her. "I can't tell you how glad I am that you were around Wednesday. Everyone was pretty shaken up when I came home that night."

"It was Kenny's quick thinking that really saved Ashley."

Maggie responded to John Pennington's easygoing smile by relaxing.

"Yeah, he's quite a young man."

Maybe too much a young man, Maggie thought. *Has Kenny had a chance to be a child? Or has he always had to help take care of his younger sister?* Maggie knew so little about her half brother and sister but was determined to change that even if she didn't plan on telling anyone who she was.

"I hear you work at Seven Oaks Hospital. That's on my route."

"Route?"

John stiffened, the smile gone. "Yeah, I drive a delivery truck and go to college at night."

"What are you studying?" Maggie sensed the subject of driving a van wasn't John's favorite.

"I'm working on a degree in business administration."

"How much longer do you have?"

"Too long. A night class here, a night class there isn't cutting it, but there isn't much else I can do."

"I can remember when I went to college. It was tough going, and I was a full-time student."

"This is my second degree. I was an engineer, but the jobs in my field dried up. Up until three years ago we lived in Texas. And before that Oklahoma and Louisiana."

"So you all moved around quite a bit?"

"Yeah, ever since we married. It was hard on Vicky. She hated leaving Seven Oaks. She was close to her family, and now her mother is gone and her father lives in Arizona with his sister. But she's happy to be back home."

"Did I hear my name in the conversation? What's this guy telling you about me, Maggie?" Vicky came up to John and sat on the arm of his chair, resting her hand on his shoulder.

"Only deep, dark secrets," John said with a laugh.

"Well, in that case, Maggie, I deny every last one of them."

She fought the impulse to blurt out Vicky's deep, dark secret. How much did John know about his wife's past? If Maggie had been a vindictive person, she would have revealed the truth in that moment, but revenge wasn't the reason she had searched for her birth mother for several years. She would still be looking if she hadn't received an anonymous tip six months ago pointing her to Seven Oaks. Maggie straightened, her hands laced tightly together.

"John, you oughta see Kane in the kitchen supervising the kids making the dessert. It's like the blind leading the blind."

"I'm not sure I want to know. What's the dessert?" John asked, putting his hand on Vicky's arm and rubbing it up and down.

"Guess."

"Has to be something chocolate."

"You know Kane and your children well."

Maggie rose suddenly, startling both John and Vicky. Wide-eyed, Maggie frantically tried to think of a logical reason to stand. "I need to use your restroom."

"First door on the right," Vicky said.

Inside the bathroom with the door closed, Maggie felt safe. She turned on the water and splashed some on her face. Looking up in the mirror, she fingered the cameo. The turmoil she felt was there in the dull flatness of her brown eyes, which shone with tears. "I can't go through with this charade. I'm going to tell her tonight and have it out. I'll demand answers to my questions, then get out of here. Go back to St. Louis where I belong. Then I won't have to worry about who killed Henry Payne."

But it will destroy any chance I have of getting to know my brother and sister. She remembered Ashley cowering behind Kane in the bedroom. Maggie wanted to break through her sister's shell; she wanted to help Kenny be a boy, not a young man at the age of eleven.

Gripping the counter, Maggie stared at herself in the mirror, fighting for that decisive determination to go back in there and continue with her original plan. She blinked, a lone tear rolling down her cheek. She furiously wiped it away. She would get to know the Penningtons, learn about them and then leave. She wouldn't cry any more tears for what she couldn't have—a loving family.

When she reentered the living room, everyone was in there, talking, laughing. When they noticed her, they stopped and stared at her, secretive smiles on their faces. A deep ache at how much an outsider she was in her own mother's home slowed her heartbeat.

Struggling to keep her lonely feelings under control, Maggie looked at Kane. "Did something happen that I should know about?"

His expression was pure innocence as he shook his head. "We were discussing the quickly approaching summer and what the kids are going to do."

"I used to go camping with my dad. Do you two like to camp?" Memories of the time spent with her adoptive dad on those outings would always be treasured.

"Yeah! We should go camping, Dad!" Kenny's eyes gleamed with enthusiasm. "We could fish for our dinner."

Vicky held up her hand. "I draw the line at eating fish. I've never been able to cook them."

Just like me. How else are we similar? The question disturbed Maggie. "My dad was so excited to teach me to fish, but he couldn't believe it when I caught a big one and then immediately threw it back into the lake. I never went fishing again. I couldn't stand to catch them when I wasn't going to eat them. I know they're good for you, but I can't stand the taste."

"Oh, I think you and I are gonna get along great. Kenny, there are other things to do during the summer vacation than camping and fishing. There's an art camp at the university I was thinking of enrolling you in."

"I love to draw!" Kenny peered at his sister. "What about Ashley? She'll need something to do."

"How about gymnastics?" Vicky asked her youngest child.

"Yes! I wanna fly through the air."

Vicky laughed and said, "You might not exactly fly, but I think you'll like it." Glancing at her watch, she stood. "Time to eat. My lasagna at this very moment is at its peak of perfection. Wait five minutes, and I'm not responsible for its contents."

At the huge round oak table at one end of the living room, Maggie sat between Kane and Kenny. Vicky was directly across from her, and every time Maggie peered up, she was drawn to the older woman. *I think you and I are gonna get along great.* The words kept repeating themselves in Maggie's mind. She shored up her resolve not to get close to Vicky.

Making herself look away from her birth mother, Maggie glanced at Kane. His expression was guarded as his gaze narrowed on her and probed beneath her own reserved look. A smile touched his eyes, as though he sensed her discomfort and he felt it was his job to put her at ease. She responded with a slow uplifting of the corners of her mouth. She forced herself to concentrate on the conversation flowing around her.

"I'm hoping that Maggie will come to my classes on Wednesday night," Vicky said, passing the basket of freshly baked rolls to John.

"I want to come, Mommy. I like to watch you cook." Ashley stuffed a forkful into her mouth.

"Not this time, sweetheart. Class doesn't get over until ten o'clock. Way past your bedtime."

Ashley stuck out her lower lip, disappointment clear in her expression.

"I promise we'll cook something next Saturday after we clean house."

"Really?"

Vicky nodded, lavishing butter all over her roll. "I was about your age when my mother started teaching me how to cook. It's about time I began passing all my family recipes along to you, Ashley. After all, us women folk have to keep the family traditions going."

Tension whipped down Maggie's length. She clenched her napkin, twisting the cotton fabric into a tight ball. She bit the inside of her cheek to keep from saying anything she would regret. Her hand trembled as she reached for her iced tea. She drank half the glass of cold liquid, amazed that she didn't drop it.

When she placed it back on the table, she caught Kane staring at her. She hoped her pain wasn't reflected in her eyes, but she wasn't good at hiding her innermost thoughts long from people. She lowered her gaze and concentrated on finishing her meal even though the delicious food suddenly tasted like cardboard and settled like a rock in her stomach.

As she took her last bite of lasagna, she noticed Kane slip from his chair and head into the kitchen. A moment later he reappeared with a covered platter. He lifted the top to reveal a plate full of chocolate cupcakes.

Kenny thrust out his chest. "I made them, and Uncle Kane helped with the icing. They're for you."

Maggie swallowed the lump rising in her throat. "They are?"

"Yep. I wanted to welcome you to the building. Mom didn't have to help me at all. The icing is Uncle Kane's special recipe."

Maggie swung her regard to Kane. "It is? You cook?"

"It was that or starve."

"Well, I'm honored." Maggie picked up the nearest cupcake and peeled off the paper.

"I licked the bowl," Ashley piped in, snatching one from the plate as she passed it.

"That's the most important job," Maggie said, taking a bite of the cupcake, sweet icing melting in her mouth. "Mmm. This is delicious. The whole meal was. I have to confess that I'm not a good cook, so it's nice to get a home-cooked meal every once and a while."

"You should take Vicky up on her offer. You couldn't learn from a better teacher." Kane popped the last of his dessert into his mouth. "She's who I learned from. In fact, I'm still learning."

"I think Kane has been responsible for sending me half my students." Vicky scooted back her chair. "Time to clean up this mess. Kenny, Ashley, clear the table please."

"I'd like to help with the dishes," Maggie said before she realized she was committing herself to being alone with Vicky.

"You don't have to. You're our guest." Vicky gathered up several plates from the table.

Guest, not family. Maggie forced a smile to her lips. "I want to help." The quicker she discovered what she had come to Seven Oaks for the quicker she could get on with her life somewhere else.

"Then sure."

"Kane, that's our cue to retire to the living room before my wife ropes us into helping, too." John pushed back his chair and rose.

"I won't argue with that." Kane watched Maggie disappear into the kitchen. At odd times he had felt her tension as though it were a palpable force emanating from her. She was wound tighter than a coil. He got the feeling it went beyond Henry's murder.

In the living room John sat in his lounge chair while Kane took a seat on the couch.

"Maggie seems like a nice lady." When Kane didn't say anything, John slid him a glance. "Not a bad-looking woman either, wouldn't you say?"

A vision of her beauty flashed into Kane's mind. Not bad looking was putting it mildly, he thought as he pictured Maggie, her chocolate-colored eyes, her full lips curved in a smile. He knew she was trouble, that she would shatter any peace of mind he had finally found, but he was having the hardest time staying away from her.

"Kane?"

Kane blinked, pushing her image from his thoughts. "I'm not saying anything. I know how you like to twist things around."

"Who? Me?"

"What about that lady in one of your classes that you tried to fix me up with?"

John held up his hand. "Okay, so that was a disaster. You're a good friend. I want you to be happy. You need to move on. Ruth wasn't the right woman for you. There's one out there for you."

"Don't." The breath in Kane's lungs expanded, causing his chest to constrict. Happy. The bomb blast that took his leg was a constant reminder of how quickly his life could change. No matter how hard he tried, he didn't have control of that life. And Ruth's desertion only confirmed that.

"Kane—"

"Look, John, I'm happy with the way things are going right now."

John's eyebrows came together in a deep frown. "I'm glad one of us is. That scare with Ashley really frightened Vicky. She never liked working, and now every morning when she leaves, I see a look on her face that makes me feel I've let her down. But we don't have the money for her to be home with the children. I don't know what to do anymore."

"That accident could happen anywhere, anytime. Besides, you don't have to pay me the rent. I don't need it."

"No, if I can't feed and take care of my family, what kind of man am I? As it is, you only charge me half what the other tenants pay. I can't accept any more charity—even from you."

"You saved my life."

"I did what anyone in the situation we faced in Iraq would have done. You don't owe me anything."

Kane started to say something else when Kenny and Ashley came bounding into the room. John turned his attention to his children. Kane wished John would let him help more, but when John had lost his job four years ago then ended up going to Iraq, it had devastated him. He and Vicky had almost divorced but somehow had pulled things together enough to move back to Seven Oaks when he returned to the United States and begin a new life.

Kane thought and remembered returning to his old life after he'd healed from his injury in the war. He'd had to let go of the plans he'd had with Ruth to marry and have a family.

"Uncle Kane." Grinning, Ashley pulled on his hand. "Please read me a bedtime story."

"Do I have to read that same story about the princess?"

"It's my favorite. Please." She stared up at him while wrapping her arms about his leg.

Kane laughed as he swung Ashley up onto his shoulders. "The only thing I can say to that is yes. Let's go see how Princess Alexa gets out of trouble this time."

Maggie heard Ashley giggling and smiled.

"It's good to hear Ashley so happy," Vicky said, sighing.

"Ever since I've had to work longer hours, she's been more with-drawn than usual. She's even started sucking her thumb again."

Another burst of laughter wafted to Maggie.

"Kane sure has a way with those two," Vicky said as she handed Maggie a plate to dry.

"Kane?"

"I can tell that giggle. He's riding her around on his shoulders. She loves it. He's quite a guy." Vicky slanted a look toward Maggie as though waiting for her to make some kind of comment about Kane. "Too bad he doesn't have children of his own. He would make a great father."

Maggie concentrated on making sure the plate was bone dry.

"He's been alone too long."

Maggie's curiosity got the better of her. This was her chance to pump Vicky for information about Kane. "I understand he was engaged once."

"I'm glad he didn't marry Ruth. She wasn't good for him, but he couldn't see that." Vicky stopped washing and faced Maggie. "Kane doesn't talk much about Ruth. I probably shouldn't have said anything, but I think it's about time he got on with his life. Meet some nice woman, settle down, have kids."

"Why tell me?" Maggie felt Vicky's gaze on her, but she stared out the window over the sink.

"Like most, I judge people on first impressions. I like you, Maggie. You would be good for Kane. And besides, you have Kenny's stamp of approval, and he's one sharp kid."

I like you, Maggie. She tried to swallow past the lump in her throat, but it was lodged so tightly. She needed to change the subject and quickly searched her mind for a safer topic. "Is your cooking class still open?"

"To you, yes. Have you decided to take the class?"

"After tasting your lasagna, I'm envious. I'm probably a hopeless case, but yes, I would like to give it a try."

"Great! I'll sign you up, and we can go to class together. No sense in both of us driving with the cost of gas being so high."

Maggie finished drying the last piece of china, trying to slow the rapid beat of her heart. Suddenly the idea of spending so much time with Vicky disarmed her more than Maggie had thought possible. *This was what you wanted,* she told herself. Yes, but couldn't she have just given Vicky a questionnaire to fill out? Surely that would be a less painful way to find out what she wanted to know.

"This is gonna be fun. Lately I haven't had much time for women friends. I realize talking with you that I've missed those friendships. Sometimes there are things you just can't talk to a man about. For some reason I feel a kinship with you." Vicky laughed, waving her hand in the air. "I guess that sounds funny to you, but it must be because of what you did for Ashley. I'll never be able to thank you enough for that."

"This dinner and your cheesecake were thanks enough," Maggie choked out, pivoting away.

"Well, I could debate that, but I'll spare you. I'm just glad you're right across the hall."

With her back to Vicky, Maggie took her time hanging up the towel on the hook. Tears were threatening to fill her eyes. She couldn't let Vicky see them. How would she ever explain them? she wondered frantically, desperate to get her emotions in check.

Maggie glanced at the clock on the wall. "Oh! Look at the time. I have a full day tomorrow. I'd better call it a night." She kept her face averted for as long as possible. When her gaze finally touched Vicky's, her control slipped further away. "Thanks for the lovely dinner."

Maggie hurried from the kitchen, said a few words to John on her way to the front door and was out in the hall before her vision blurred. She felt as though she was coming apart atom by atom, and there was no way she could stop it. Inside her apartment, she made her way to her bathroom.

I like Vicky. I enjoy the camaraderie. For a while I felt I belonged to her family.

With that realization came the guilt, the confusion. Maggie stood before her mirror over the sink, trying to pull herself together. She had thought coming to Seven Oaks would be so much easier than it was turning out to be. She had thought back in St. Louis all she had to do was waltz into Vicky's life, have her questions answered and move on with her own life.

Not so.

The tears began to flow. As they streamed down her cheeks, she realized she hadn't unpacked the tissues yet, so she grabbed the toilet paper and dabbed at her face. Still, she cried. Needing more tissue before leaving to head into her bedroom, she decided to take the whole roll with her. It might be one of those nights where she finally let go of the tight restraints on her emotions. Through the film of tears, she fumbled with the dispenser and dropped the metal rod. It skated across the tile, coming apart. Inside, a small, black rectangular object skidded from its protective nest.

A flash drive hidden in the toilet paper holder?

SIX

When a rap came at the front door, Maggie continued to stare at the small black flash drive. The pounding continued, and she realized she wouldn't be able to ignore whoever kept knocking. Sucking in several calming breaths, she stooped and picked up the computer device, similar to one she'd used before but not hers.

Whose then? Henry's?

"Maggie!" Kane's worried tone prodded her into action.

She hurried from the bathroom, swiping her cheeks to rid her face of all traces of her tears. Her heartbeat matched the insistent pounding as she touched the knob. She wrenched open the door.

Kane stood in the lighted hallway, his concerned expression skimming over her features. "What's going on? Are you crying?"

"It's nothing." She gestured as though to dismiss the last several hours.

Kane captured her hand as he took a step forward. She moved back. Shutting the door with a nudge of his foot, he released her and ran his finger gently across her cheek.

"I'd say that was a tear, and I doubt you'd cry over nothing."

She showed him the flash drive. "I found this in my bathroom hidden in the metal roller of the toilet paper dispenser."

One eyebrow rose. "And that made you cry?"

"It isn't mine, which means it must be the prior occupant's."

"You think Henry hid it there? Why?"

"Good question. I wonder what's on this."

"There's only one way to find out. Let's look. If it's Henry's then we'll give it to David in case there's some kind of evidence on it. Do you have a computer? If not, I do downstairs."

"Yeah, I set up my home office in the spare bedroom." She pointed toward the hallway.

"Where Henry did."

The thought bothered her more than it should, but with what she had been hearing about the man, he wasn't a nice person. She didn't like having anything in common with him. Living in the same apartment was bad enough.

Inside the spare bedroom she quickly crossed to her desk and sat in the padded chair. She ran her hand across the polished piece of walnut that Kane had used to make the piece of furniture. "This is beautiful. Edwina said something about you retiring from the university to work full-time making furniture."

"I'm at peace when I create a piece. My heart isn't in my job at the school. All the uproar over Henry's murder has just proven that to me." Kane pulled a chair up next to her. "When I came back from Iraq, I needed to do something familiar, so I went back to my old job, but I quickly realized I don't want to do it any longer."

"Hence the new occupation." Maggie booted up her laptop. "I'm thankful I love what I do. Helping people regain their speech abilities after a stroke fulfills me." Feeling his gaze on her, she connected with it. "When are you going to retire?"

"At the end of the school year. I informed Dr. Johnson, the president of Seven Oaks University, last week."

"How did he take it?"

"Not well. He doesn't like change."

"Not many people do, but life is full of changes." Boy, did she know that! Since her adoptive father had died, her life had been one series of changes after another.

Kane stuck the flash drive into the USB port. "If this belongs to Henry, let's hope it will give us some answers. I'm tired of Dr. Johnson breathing down my neck as if I caused all this uproar."

Maggie clicked on the only file folder that popped up. When a screen came up asking for a password, she groaned. "Nothing can be easy. Do you have any suggestions what Henry's password is?"

"Well, we could try the obvious ones, but there's always a chance this isn't Henry's. Try science and science department. Or Seven Oaks University."

After typing in those words and nothing happening, she looked at Kane. "What's his birthday?"

He shrugged. "I should have it on his application he filled out when he wanted to rent the apartment. But truthfully Henry isn't an obvious kind of guy." He stared off in space, a frown wrinkling his brow. Suddenly a smile spread across his face. "I may have a solution. We could be here days trying to figure it out, but I know someone who is great with computers. As a teen he hacked into the high school network and changed some friends' grades. He might know how to get around the password. He takes care of the computers at the university."

"Who? Let's call him."

"It's Bradley Quinn. You met him at Edwina's the other evening." Rising, Kane headed into the living room and dialed information, then placed a call to Bradley. When he hung up, he faced Maggie. "He's coming right over. We'll meet him down in my apartment. I'll get Henry's application in case we need it."

Maggie returned to the bedroom and grabbed the flash drive, then met Kane by the front door. A few minutes later she sat at his desk in a corner of his living room, staring at the screen while Kane retrieved the application. She tried a few more words—apartment 2A, the address of the building, stamp collector. Nothing worked, and she didn't know Henry well enough to come up with any more words.

When Kane entered with a paper in hand, she said, "Tell me about Henry."

"He used people." Kane took the chair next to Maggie. "But that won't help us figure out his password. Let's try his birth date."

After Kane recited it, Maggie typed in the numbers then tried using the month spelled out. Neither opened the file on the flash drive. "Okay, besides stamp collecting, what else did Henry do in his free time?"

"He read a lot."

"What kind of books?"

"Thrillers."

"That figures," Maggie mumbled while inputting words having to do with that pastime. "Does anyone in the building know Henry better than you?"

"Edwina might, and I've gotten the impression that Vicky, John and Henry went to high school together here in Seven Oaks. They all grew up here and are only a few years apart in age."

"Anyone else? Maybe someone at the university?"

"Dr. Johnson and Henry grew up together."

"So they're friends?" Maggie hadn't gotten the idea that John or Vicky had been friends with Henry.

Kane plowed his fingers through his hair. "Not exactly. On

the surface they gave that impression, but I don't think they had much to do with each other since Henry moved back to Seven Oaks."

"If Bradley can't help us, I could talk to Edwina while you see Vicky and John about Henry."

"Speaking of them, why did you leave so fast this evening?"

"Left fast? Whatever gave you that impression?"

"I came back to the living room to find you were gone, and John told me you hurried out the door after helping Vicky clean up."

Maggie stared down at the keyboard. "It was late. I thought it was time to go. I…"

"Why were you crying? Did something happen at John and Vicky's that upset you?"

Everything, she wanted to shout but didn't. She honed in on one of the myriad things that bothered her about the evening and said, "I hated to see Ashley so shy and afraid of me."

"She's that way with everyone. It took her a year to warm up to me. But why would that make you cry?" His assessing gaze studied her.

"Because she reminded me of myself at that age."

"You, shy?"

"Yes, painfully so." She looked away from the intensity in his eyes that threatened to peel away the layers of her defense. "I was adopted twice. Once as a baby until the state took me away from the couple for neglect and abuse. I have no memory of that because I wasn't even two when it happened. That's just what my second adoptive father told me when I asked questions about my past. I lived in a series of foster homes for several years until I could be adopted again. Then it took over a year before I was."

"I'm sorry."

"Don't be. I learned to fend for myself at a young age. It's made—" A buzzing sound halted Maggie's words.

"That must be Bradley." Kane crossed to the security panel and pressed a button. "Kane McDowell here."

"Hey, it's Bradley. I brought a program that should do the trick."

Kane buzzed him in, then made his way to his door and opened it. "Maggie, we'll finish our discussion later." Shortly after, the tall, thin young man entered Kane's apartment.

"Did you forget a password, Kane?" Bradley asked, shrugging out of a light jacket.

"Not exactly." Kane gestured toward where Maggie sat.

Bradley's gaze lit upon her, widening slightly. He covered the distance to the desk. "Miss Ridgeway. Nice to see you again. Is this the flash drive?"

"Yes. I can't get into the file on it. It's protected by a password."

"Have you tried all the ones you usually use?"

"I've tried everything I can think of."

Bradley sat where Kane had while he took up a position behind Maggie. Angling the computer toward him, the young man began working to recover the password by using a program he'd brought. "This may take some time. Make yourselves comfortable."

Kane made some coffee for them, then sat with Maggie to wait.

A few hours later Bradley said, "Got it. It's Sam Maples— all one word, lowercase." He clicked on the file as Maggie reached to retrieve the computer. "I didn't know you knew the new chair of the science department."

"I don't. I found this flash drive in my apartment. It wasn't mine, but I didn't know whose it was." Maggie pulled the laptop toward her.

"Then this must be Henry's. Maybe he kept information about the professors in his department." Bradley relaxed back in his chair as though he wasn't going anywhere.

As Maggie opened the file, Kane turned to the young man. "Thanks for coming on such short notice."

Frowning, Bradley stood. "If you need any more help, I'm just a phone call away."

"I'll keep that in mind." Kane headed for the door.

While Kane let Bradley out of the apartment, Maggie clicked on the first photo in the folder. An older man embraced a young woman in what looked like a classroom.

"What's on the file?" Kane asked when he came back to the desk.

"Is this Sam Maples?" She showed him the screen.

"Yes."

"Is that a student?"

"It's hard to tell at that angle. I can't see her face well, but I do know it isn't his wife. His wife's his age."

Maggie opened the next picture file. The photo depicted a young woman with long auburn hair kissing Dr. Maples in his office.

"It could be a student. She's about the right age." Stationed behind her, Kane leaned forward to get a better view.

"There's another I can open." The third one, taken as though the person with the camera was standing outside a window, showed Sam and the same redhead in a passionate embrace. Maggie shifted to glance back at Kane, his close proximity threatening her concentration. "Why would Henry have these pictures?"

"Maybe he used them to hold over Sam." Kane sank into the chair next to her.

"So if Henry was blackmailing Sam for some reason, that could be a motive for killing him."

"Yep."

"I'm beginning to see why you don't think Henry is a nice man."

"We'd better let David check into that. I'll call him. Knowing him, he'll come over tonight for the flash drive."

She closed down the files in the folder and removed the device. "Good. The sooner this is resolved the sooner I'll feel safe." Pushing to her feet at the same time Kane did, she bumped against him. She stepped back, but not before her heartbeat quickened.

He clasped her arms, focusing her attention on him. A grin tilted his mouth upward as he cupped her face. "David's good at his job. He won't railroad Sam because there are only a few leads. Leave it to him."

"Okay." But curiosity whittled its way into her mind. Had they found the murderer?

"Are you sure you don't mind watching Kenny and Ashley?" Vicky asked Maggie in the middle of her living room on Saturday morning.

"No, I told you Wednesday night after cooking class I didn't mind watching them when something comes up. Besides, this gives me an excuse not to finish unpacking and to check out the new park a few blocks away."

"Ashley will love that. The city has finally updated all the playground equipment. She has been asking me to take her, but I haven't had the time." Vicky snatched up her purse. "I don't usually have to work on Saturday, and I should be back by noon."

Maggie waved her hands. "Go. Don't worry. We're gonna have a picnic and be back about two. That'll give you some time to unwind before the kids descend on you."

"Ashley is in her room getting dressed," Vicky said,

heading for the door, "and Kenny is downstairs helping Kane with some sanding."

"Does Kenny want to go to the park?"

"Ask him. I never know with him. One day he wants to be all grown up and the next he doesn't. But he doesn't play like he used to. He doesn't say so, but I think he's worrying about something."

"Do you think it's because of Henry's murder?"

Standing in the entrance to the apartment, Vicky shrugged, an intensity to her expression. "He was acting strange before that, but I'm sure that hasn't helped. What happened to you hasn't helped either."

When she had mentioned Henry's name, Vicky had flinched and anger glinted in her eyes. As she suspected, someone else who hadn't liked Henry. "Hopefully that's over. Everything this past week has been peaceful although David hasn't come up with any solid leads. Don't worry about us. We're gonna have some fun."

As Vicky left, Maggie thought about what David had told Kane after checking into what was on the flash drive. The detective had talked with Sam Maples. He'd also been surprised by the photos Henry had of him and couldn't give an explanation of their origin. David hadn't had enough to charge him with anything. The young woman in the picture was of legal age, and Dr. Maples' wife had given him an alibi for the night of the murder. But the detective would keep Sam Maples on the list of suspects.

"Is Mommy gone?"

Ashley's quiet words grounded Maggie in the present. She swung around to face the little girl, who was dressed in jeans and a pink T-shirt, her hair pulled back in a ponytail. Again Maggie had the overpowering urge to sweep her sister up into her arms and give her all the love she had bottled up inside her. Instead, she smiled at the child and said, "Yeah, she just left."

Ashley hung back by the entrance into the hallway. "She said you were gonna take me and Kenny to the park."

"Yes, I even brought some food for a picnic and a Frisbee to play with."

"Where's my brother?"

"At Kane's. We're going down to get him." Maggie picked up the backpack she had the food and Frisbee in and then held her hand out for Ashley.

Slowly the child advanced across the room, but she didn't stop where Maggie stood. She kept going and opened the door into the hallway.

Sighing, Maggie slung the backpack over her shoulders and followed Ashley down to the basement. By the time Maggie reached the workshop, Kane had let the little girl inside and waited for Maggie in the corridor. He lounged against the wall, his arms casually crossed over his T-shirt-clad chest, sympathy in his expression.

When she neared, he whispered, "She'll come around. Do you want company at the park? I could use a break from working since six this morning."

Without his presence, she wasn't sure how close Ashley would let her get. "Are you sure?"

"Very. Kenny's been talking about checking out the monkey bars."

"Great."

Kane turned back into his workshop. "Are you two ready to go play? I am."

"Yep," both of them answered him at the same time.

Fifteen minutes later, Maggie stood next to Kane near the multicolored play structure with slides, tunnels, climbing surfaces and two forts. The second they hit the park both children ran toward the equipment to join kids of all ages testing out the elaborate system.

The grin on Ashley's face sent joy through Maggie. Her sister found some children her age and was playing with them in one of the forts. Kenny met some friends from school and they were scaling the small rock wall.

Maggie spied an empty bench. "Let's sit. I don't think there's much for us to do but watch."

"After sanding for hours, I'm game. Watching sounds nice."

Maggie took a seat, placing her backpack between them as though she needed that physical barrier to keep her on track with her mission. Kane had a way of diverting her attention with one simple smile. "Have you heard anything else from David? Earlier this morning when I had breakfast with Edwina, she thought David was out of leads other than to keep an eye on Dr. Maples."

"I'm still trying to figure out why Henry would want to blackmail Sam."

"Maybe he wasn't."

"Then why did Henry have those photos hidden on a flash drive?"

"Because he's a strange man?" Maggie lifted her shoulder in a shrug, at a loss to what or who was behind Henry's murder.

A little blond-haired boy raced by them toward the big slide. A petite woman, overdressed for the park in a black pantsuit, stopped near Maggie's side of the bench, calling out, "Tyler, slow down."

Kane glanced at the woman and smiled. "Beth, it's nice to see you here. Is that your son?" He pointed toward the child who clambered up the ladder to the tallest slide.

"Yes. He was eager to come to the park, and it looks like half the children in Seven Oaks decided to do the same thing."

When Tyler stood up on the top of the slide, Beth shouted, "Tyler, get down now." Moving toward the playground equipment, she peered back at Kane. "Sorry I can't talk. I've got to keep a close eye on my son." For a second, the woman's gaze skimmed over Maggie before she faced forward and marched toward the slide.

"Who's she?" Maggie watched the petite woman get her son down from the slide and direct him toward the tunnels where Ashley was crawling through with another little girl.

"Dr. Beth Warren was recently promoted to dean of women at the university. Enough about her. Isn't it time for lunch?" Kane tapped the backpack sitting between them. "So what have you brought? Hopefully food."

"Lunch. I have enough for you, too."

He lifted the knapsack. "What did you put in here? The whole refrigerator."

"Ashley and Kenny are growing children, and I noticed last Sunday night they ate a lot. I wanted to make sure I had enough for them."

"When are we going to eat?"

She chuckled. "Are you hungry?"

"Did I tell you I got up and started working at six this morning and forgot to eat breakfast? Yes, I'm starved, and I'm sure Kenny worked up quite an appetite, too."

"Is that your way of telling me to set up lunch?"

"Yep. I'll go get the kids while you find a place for us to eat." He stood quickly and hurried toward the play equipment.

Taking her cue from Kane, Maggie gathered the backpack and checked out the park looking for a place to set up her feast. To the left was an area with lush grass and several large oaks that offered some shade. But in the middle was a wide-open space where they could throw the Frisbee. She staked out a place under one of the trees near the field. As she spread a king-size blanket over the ground, Kane and the children approached her.

"We're eating here, too?" Kenny plopped down near Maggie. "Neat!"

Ashley stood on the edge of the blanket slightly behind Kane, who had sat slowly, stretching out both legs. It took all Maggie's control to tamp down her anger that she hadn't been a part of her sister's life from the beginning. Each time Ashley shied away from her, her heart twisted.

"What are we having?" Kenny tried to peek into the backpack.

"Your mom told me you two like ham and cheese sandwiches." Maggie dug into the backpack and pulled out a sandwich for Kenny then Ashley.

The little girl stared at it a moment then hesitantly took it from Maggie, mumbling, "Thanks."

As Kane grabbed his, he said, "C'mon, princess. Sit and join us."

Reluctantly Ashley did, flanked on both sides by Kane and Kenny.

"I brought lemonade and tropical punch. Which do you all want?" Maggie removed several cans.

Kenny and Kane took the lemonade while Ashley grabbed the tropical punch. For the next ten minutes, the two kids stuffed their mouths and drained their drinks as if they were in a race.

When Kenny finished, he squeezed his leftover foil into a ball and tossed it at Ashley. She grinned and did the same with hers.

"I have a Frisbee you two can throw around if you want." Maggie retrieved it from the backpack.

Kenny snatched it and leaped to his feet. "C'mon, Ashley. I'll show you how it's done."

"Stay near," Maggie said as they left, jogging toward the open area.

Maggie watched them play. For all his complaining about Ashley, Kenny did a good job as a big brother. She wanted the chance to be a big sister.

"Maggie, they're good kids. You don't need to worry they'd go off without saying something first."

"I'm not worried." Maggie kept her gaze trained on the children.

"Then why the concerned look?"

Ashley finally caught the Frisbee in midair and pumped her arm in victory. Maggie smiled and shifted her attention to Kane.

"I thought Sunday night at dinner there was a little softening toward me on Ashley's part. But today you would think we were strangers meeting for the first time."

"You should have seen her with Henry. He lived across the hall for two years, and she would go to great lengths to avoid him." He took a swig of his drink. "She'll come around. She got separated from Vicky once at a department store. It was traumatic for Ashley as well as Vicky. They found Ashley cowering behind some clothes crying."

"When was that?"

"Two years ago. Things changed after that. She would hardly leave Vicky's side for months."

"How long have you known them?"

"Three and a half years. When my reserve unit was called up for the war, I met John Pennington in Iraq. We became friends because we're both from Seven Oaks although he'd been living in other places for years."

"When did you convert the house into an apartment building?" Maggie finished the last bite of her sandwich.

"Six years ago."

"I understand it's been a popular place to rent, that you don't have a lot of vacancies."

"True. When I came back from the war, I had one. I contacted John in Iraq, explaining that I had a place for him and his family to live if he wanted to return to Seven Oaks. He'd talked about doing that while we were serving together. He saved my life. I wanted to repay him."

"He saved your life?"

"Yes, he'd pulled me from a bombed building before the ceiling collapsed on me."

Edwina had hinted at a close relationship between John and Kane, forged by the war they had served in together. Although she was getting to know Kane, there was still so much she didn't know. And she shouldn't spend her emotional energy trying to figure him out.

"I was discharged early because I was injured from the blast. That's behind me now. But there isn't much I wouldn't do for the Penningtons," Kane said in a fervent tone. "Even if I hadn't had a vacancy, I would have found a place for them to live. I owe John."

"The house is beautiful. I can see why you don't have much trouble renting your apartments." She spread her arms wide. "Just look at me. Even with Henry's murder, I was on your doorstep before your ad appeared in the newspaper."

"I've only had two vacancies in the six years since I converted the mansion—the family in the Pennington's and the person who had the place before Henry. Charles Wentworth up and left suddenly."

"He did?" *Was the apartment jinxed?* The thought chilled her. "Where did he go?"

Kane shrugged. "Beats me. He left behind his five hundred dollar deposit. He was Dr. Johnson's assistant. Vicky got that job after Wentworth left."

"Was 2A vacant long?"

"No, only a day. Henry appeared and moved in immediately. He'd just gotten the job as head of the science department and needed a place to stay. The old department head had died after a short illness. The school year had started, and things were hectic."

"Where did Henry live before coming to town?"

"At a university in Nashville."

Maggie saw Beth and Tyler walking away from the playground and smiled at the petite woman. Kane waved at the pair, and Beth detoured toward them.

"I'm sorry I didn't get a chance to speak much earlier." Beth stopped near Kane, her gaze shifting to Maggie. "I'm Beth Warren."

"Maggie Ridgeway."

Tyler tugged on his mother's arm. She glanced down and the boy asked, "Can I go play with Ashley and her brother?"

After the child dashed off, Maggie peered at Beth. "He knows Kenny and Ashley?"

"Ashley and Tyler are in the same kindergarten class."

Kane scooted over next to Maggie. "Sit. Join us. It looks like the kids are playing together."

Beth stared at her son for a few long seconds then sank down on the blanket. "With all that's happened lately, I'm glad."

"You mean Henry's murder," Maggie said, spying Bradley Quinn striding toward them.

Beth frowned. "Yeah."

The woman's look closed off any further discussion of the subject of Henry. Obviously Beth Warren wasn't a fan of Henry's either.

"Beth, I'm sorry I'm late." Bradley paused next to where the woman sat.

She smiled up at Bradley. "That's okay. I've been talking to Kane and Maggie. Have you met Maggie?"

Bradley folded his long length beside Beth. "Yes, she lives in Henry's old apartment."

Beth's eyes widened. "Oh. I didn't know."

"Did anything pan out about the flash drive? I assume you turned it over to David." Bradley clasped Beth's hand between them.

"He hasn't said anything to me." Kane stuffed the trash into the backpack. "Have you heard anything? He's your cousin."

"Nope."

"What flash drive?" Beth looked at the man next to her.

"Maggie found a flash drive in her apartment. It wasn't hers so they speculated it was Henry's. There was a password-protected file on it."

Beth swung her attention to Maggie. "Where in the world was it? I thought they had cleaned out all Henry's possessions."

"In a toilet paper dispenser."

"Odd." Beth frowned.

"My dear, but doesn't that sound just like Henry?" Bradley slipped his arm around Beth and pulled her against him as though protecting her.

"What was on it?" Beth asked, her voice raspy. She swallowed several times.

Maggie didn't know what to say to that question. She peered at Kane, silently wanting him to intervene.

"Since Henry's murder is an ongoing investigation, we don't feel we should say anything about the flash drive's contents. David is dealing with it."

The color leached from Beth's face. She quickly averted her eyes and glanced toward her son in the open area. "We'd better go, Bradley, if we're going to take—take Tyler to the library."

Bradley stood and helped Beth to her feet. As she hurried toward her son, Bradley said, "As I said before, if you need my help anytime in the future, just call. I think it's neat being a part of Henry's murder investigation."

"What was that all about?" Maggie asked as she watched them gather Tyler and begin to walk toward the parking lot.

"Beth dated Henry when he first came to Seven Oaks. It didn't end well, and although she avoided him as much as possible, she had to work with him sometimes."

"Which makes for an uncomfortable situation." She knew that firsthand having dated a man who she had to work with at a hospital. Their breakup was one of the reasons she decided to leave St. Louis and finally come to Seven Oaks. His harassment had been difficult to dodge when he purposely pursued her at work.

"I'm glad to see she's finally dating again. She didn't for a long time after Henry broke it off."

"Do you think she was in love with Henry?"

"I guess it's possible. He could be charming to the women. He didn't want for dates." Kane's full attention riveted to her. "But she doesn't look like she's grieving his loss, so obviously she's moved on."

Maggie found the woman at the edge of the park. Tyler ran ahead to a car while Bradley and Beth hung back. Bradley grasped the petite woman's arms and drew her close. Even at a distance, Maggie felt the intensity generated from their conversation. Interesting. Would Beth have had a reason to kill Henry?

SEVEN

"Thanks for helping me set up for the housewarming party. You're a lifesaver." Maggie pulled a relish tray out of the refrigerator.

Edwina arranged the paper plates and napkins in an arc on the counter. "Didn't Vicky offer to help, too?"

"Haven't you heard the saying that too many cooks in the kitchen make for total confusion?" She'd already spent more time with Vicky than she had ever thought she would when planning to come to Seven Oaks. She certainly didn't need to add any more.

"Dear, it's spoil the broth," Edwina said with a chuckle, moving on to prepare the coffee.

"You get the picture."

"How was the picnic yesterday at the park?" Edwina loaded the coffeemaker with a filter, grounds and water, then plugged in the machine.

"It was nice. Toward the end Ashley started warming up to me. She tossed me the Frisbee a few times, and on the walk back to Twin Oaks, she didn't hide like she did on the trip to the playground."

"You're making headway. That's actually quite fast."

Fast! We're sisters. There should be much more between

us than not fleeing at my sight. "That's what Kane said to me last night."

"Last night?" Edwina's eyes gleamed. "Is there something you want to tell me?"

"No. And quit getting any ideas. There's nothing between us." *If I say it enough, it will be true.*

Maggie finished getting the last dish out of the refrigerator and turned toward Edwina. "Did you start the coffee?"

Edwina checked the machine. "Yes. It should be perking."

"I was afraid of this. It's old, and I think it got banged up during the move. I should have bought a new one the other day at the store. Do you have one I can borrow?"

"No, I only drink tea, but Henry has one. Remember? I doubt he would care that you borrowed it for the afternoon and neither will anyone else since there's no one to claim his possessions."

"I don't know. Maybe I could go to the—"

"Hush, child. I'll take care of it and be back in a sec. It's brand-new and should be used. Besides, you're only borrowing it for the afternoon."

Before Maggie could say anything, Edwina scurried away. The sound of the door closing stopped any last second protest of using a dead man's coffeepot. She swung back to the counter, laden with prepared—mostly store-bought—food.

"I came a few minutes early to see if you needed any help."

Kane's deep baritone voice surprised her. Maggie gasped and spun around to face him in the doorway into her kitchen.

He grinned. "Where's Edwina rushing off to?"

"To get Henry's coffeemaker. Mine's broke. Do you think he'll mind if I borrow it?"

"Henry? After what he's put us through, he'd better not." Kane gestured toward the trays filled with all kinds of goodies from cookies to a cheese ball. "What army is coming?"

"Okay, I may have gone overboard just a tad, but I wanted to make sure I had enough food."

His grin grew, lighting his eyes. "Yep, you have enough for three or four housewarming parties."

"Then I'll be eating leftovers for a while."

"What can I do to help?" Kane lounged against the counter.

"Nothing. I'm serving all the food in here, and whenever anyone wants something they can come grab it."

"Where did you get the punch bowl? It looks familiar."

"Vicky loaned it to me yesterday. Cups, too." Maggie turned away, busying herself straightening the celery sticks on the platter. "She said it has been in her family for two generations."

"There's no punch in it."

Maggie whirled around, hand to mouth. "Oh, no. I forgot. I need to make it."

Kane blocked her forward motion with his arm. "Let me. What do I put in the bowl?"

"Ginger ale and lime sherbet."

"That's all?"

"Yep. Even I can't mess up that recipe. I think that's why Vicky suggested it."

"So the cooking class isn't going well?"

"What makes you say that?"

"I saw you the other evening returning. You didn't look too pleased."

Maggie thought back to the lesson and ride with Vicky to the class on Wednesday night. Maggie's cooking could have been better, but her weary expression when she'd come home had probably been from an overload of playing the part of a friend to Vicky. *I'm not going to allow myself to care for the woman. Lord, I can't. Look what she did to me.*

"Just tired. Going out Wednesday night for two hours makes for a long day."

Edwina appeared in the kitchen, clutching the coffeemaker. "I've got it. It was just downstairs collecting dust. Now it's going to be put to good use." She gave it to Kane. "I don't fix coffee. You can see what happened to my last attempt." She pointed to the broken coffeepot on the counter. "You do and it's good, so I'll finish the punch for you while you make the coffee."

"Sure. That's something I can do." Kane took the machine and headed toward Maggie at the counter.

"You know Henry never had a housewarming party. In fact, he never had a party." Edwina scooped the sherbet into the ginger ale that was already in the glass bowl.

"He didn't entertain at all?" Maggie continued to arrange the vegetables around the dip bowl, aware of how close Kane was to her—another one of Edwina's manipulations. This kitchen wasn't made for three people when one was Kane.

"Only occasionally and with small groups, maybe two or three," Edwina said.

"Leave it to you to know what's going on in the building." Kane fit the prepackaged coffee down into the basket.

"It's part of my job as manager, but I'm not doing a good job lately or I'd know who broke into Maggie's apartment."

Maggie stepped closer to Kane and removed the foil from the tray of sandwiches. "You can't be on 24-7. Besides, nothing's happened this week." She was trying to be optimistic about the situation because she wasn't moving.

"I know that Vicky and her family will be the first ones through the front door for this party." Edwina dipped the ladle into the punch and tested it. "Mmm. Simple and delicious."

Kane filled the carafe with water and began to pour it into the top. He stopped before he did and put the glass pot down. Then he examined the machine. "Something's down in this taped to the side."

"What?" Maggie moved even closer to take a look.

Kane stuck his fingers into an opening and pulled out an oblong black flash drive exactly like the other one Maggie had found in the apartment. "I wonder who Henry targeted on this one."

"Call Bradley, and have him bring his program to the party in case we need it to open any files on this. It may not be anything but his tax information or something like that." But as Maggie stared at the flash drive, her excitement built. Maybe this one had information concerning the killer.

"We'll need to let David know."

"He can stay and take the drive if it proves to be anything." Maggie slipped the device into her pocket.

"This has been such a lovely housewarming." Edwina took a sip of her punch.

"Yes, I can't believe everyone came." Maggie scanned the people—a room full—still at the party after two hours. The flash drive was still safely in her pocket. Eager to discover what was on the device, she rocked back and forth on her heels.

Edwina peered at her. "The Sellmans and Bradley's parents have left. The others will soon."

"Am I that obvious?" Maggie stood still, clutching her own cup of punch.

"Only to someone with a trained eye for details."

"I'll try to be more casual as if I might not hold the key to Henry's murder in my pocket."

Kane came up behind her. "Vicky and John are leaving with Ashley and Kenny."

For a few seconds, guilt took hold of Maggie. She hadn't talked much with Vicky at the party. She'd spent a lot of time with Kenny and even Ashley, who hadn't shied away from her. On top of everything that had happened, dealing with Vicky was just too much.

"I need to say goodbye." Maggie made her way toward the couple who lived across from her. "Thanks for coming. I love the plant." She took John's hand to shake it.

When Maggie faced Vicky, her birth mother enveloped Maggie in a hug. "We need to get together more in this building. It's like a little community. Now that Henry…" Her mouth snapped closed. "I mean—"

"You don't have to explain to me about what kind of man Henry was. I imagine things are a lot more pleasant with him not living here."

Vicky blew out a breath of air. "Yes. A lot. I know it isn't nice talking about someone who is dead, but there was always so much tension when he was around."

Kenny joined them at the door. "Mom, Maggie said she would take me and Ashley to the movies one weekend. Can we go?"

Vicky looked at Maggie. "Are you sure?"

"Yes." Why did the woman keep asking her that question? Kenny and Ashley were adorable, and they were her siblings.

"Then, that's great," the older woman said to her son.

Both Kenny and Ashley beamed.

Joy spread through Maggie at seeing her brother and sister happy. She would never do anything to harm them. That was why she wouldn't say anything to Vicky about who she was. What happened twenty-eight years ago would remain a secret.

After the Penningtons left, Kyra and her son approached Maggie. "We'd better leave, too. Tomorrow is a school day, and Sean has some homework."

"Thanks for coming. The place mats are beautiful. They go great in my kitchen."

"You're welcome."

Fifteen minutes later, her apartment held only a handful of people—Bradley, David, Edwina, Kane and herself. "Let me get my laptop."

Maggie retrieved it from her office and reentered the living room. Sitting on the couch next to Kane, she opened the computer and booted it up.

After sticking the flash drive into the USB port, she announced to the group, "It's like before. The only file on the drive is password-protected."

"Let me see what I can do with it," Bradley said and took the laptop from Maggie.

When he had gotten into the file, Bradley clicked on the first document. "Strange."

Maggie grasped the computer, bringing it back to her lap. "What was the password this time?"

"Phil Johnson."

"The president of the university?" Kane leaned close to Maggie while David walked behind the couch to stand looking over her shoulder.

"What is it?" Edwina asked from a chair in front of Maggie.

"It's an old newspaper article from July 1975 about a fire. The Johnsons' house burned down during the night. The husband and wife didn't make it out alive, but their thirteen-year-old son was spending the night with a friend, Henry Payne."

"And the son was our president, Phillip Johnson?"

"The dates add up," David said, gesturing toward the other documents listed. "Open the next one."

Maggie clicked on the icon, and another article popped up on the computer screen. The headlines proclaimed the fire that killed Dr. and Mrs. Johnson was arson, but there were no suspects. "Why would Henry have this?"

"They were best friends growing up." Edwina pushed to her feet and shuffled toward the kitchen. "It was a big news story years ago. I'd forgotten all about it until now. It rocked Seven Oaks and the university because Dr. Mel Johnson was the president, and the arsonist was never found." She paused and glanced back. "Some say he made a few enemies by some decisions he made concerning the school but nothing that should have driven someone to burn his house down with him in it." Shaking her head, Edwina disappeared into the other room, mumbling, "It's sad what evil can do to a person."

The next file Maggie opened were a series of photos of two boys being boys. "Those could be of Phillip and Henry. I see the similarities."

"What's the last document?" David asked, coming around the couch to sit on Maggie's other side as Bradley rose.

She opened it. "A letter dated a few years back to Phillip Johnson, congratulating him on becoming the president of Seven Oaks University." Scanning the second paragraph, she frowned. "This is odd. 'Now I can come home, and you can welcome me to the staff with open arms. After all, what are best friends for if not to look out for each other.' Was Henry in some kind of trouble at his previous school in Nashville?"

David took the laptop and studied the letter. "I don't know, but I'm going to do some checking. I'm not sure how that will help his murder case, though."

"Maybe the person who killed Henry isn't from here. It isn't unheard of that someone comes to town and kills a person then leaves." Bradley paced in front of the coffee table. "Whatever it is, cousin, I'm sure you'll figure it out. I'd better be going. I have a date tonight."

"Ah, with Beth Warren?" Maggie asked, grasping the computer when David slid it back to her. She removed the flash drive and gave it to the detective.

"I don't kiss and tell." Bradley winked at her, then left the apartment.

"It's nice to see him dating after what happened with his last girlfriend." David pocketed the flash drive. "Thanks for this." At the front door, he stopped and faced Maggie. "Do you think there are any more hidden in here?"

"I don't know. I doubt it. Technically this one wasn't in here, but in Henry's possessions."

"I'll get with Aunt Edwina and go through Henry's boxes. Maybe another one is stuffed in something of his. Of course, I'm not sure how these flash drives are connected to his murder."

"And one box was taken from the storeroom. No telling what was in that," Kane said, rubbing his hand along his nape. "I just hope you can solve it soon. I won't feel better until you do."

After David left, Maggie hurried into the kitchen and stopped Edwina from cleaning up. "I appreciate all your help, but you deserve to sit, not work."

"Dr. Mel Johnson was president when I came to work for the library at the school. I hadn't thought about his death in years, but it has brought back painful memories. He was a good man who had elevated the university's status."

"Phillip is doing well, too." Kane filled a mug with the last of the coffee. "Our recruitment among the elite high school students is good."

"But what will this murder do to that?"

"The murderer will be found, and all this negative publicity will die down. In the meantime, it's business as usual in my department." Relaxing back against the counter, he sipped his drink.

Murder. Flash drives. The dynamics of a prestigious university. It was getting to be too much for Maggie. Her head pounded with tension. "Edwina, thank you for your help, but I'll take care of all this." She spread her arms wide to indicate the leftover food and dirty dishes.

"I'm not going to argue with you on this." Weariness etched

Edwina's wrinkled face. "I'm tired and could use a nap." She padded toward the door. "Your party was a success."

Silence descended after the older woman's departure. While massaging her temples, Maggie closed her eyes for a few seconds.

"Do you want me to go, too?" Kane said, surprisingly close to her.

She gasped, not having heard him move. "You don't have to stay. It would probably do me some good to throw myself into cleaning up rather than thinking about Henry's murder one more minute."

"Then let me help you. Here." He turned her until her back was to him, then clasped her shoulders and began kneading them.

His strong hands worked the tension from her. She concentrated on their action, and before long nothing else mattered. She wanted to melt back against Kane, but with an effort, she remained still.

"Don't let this get to you," Kane whispered close to her ear, his breath fanning her skin.

"I'm trying not to let it get to me."

His hands stopped and slipped from her shoulders. "Let David do his job."

She spun around, coming within inches of Kane. "I can't. I've never been one to let someone else solve my problems."

"What problems?"

"Ever since that intruder invaded my home, it has become my problem."

One corner of his mouth tipped upward. "As I told you, it's mine, too." Kane cupped her face, his mouth hovering over hers. "We're in this together. We'll do our own investigating into Sam Maples and Phillip Johnson."

"Don't forget about Henry at his old university."

His smile became full-fledged. "I know the admissions director at that school. I'll give him a call and see what he has to say about Henry."

His breath, laced with coffee and chocolate from the dessert tray he'd frequented during the party, teased her senses. She drew in a lungful of the scent. His fingers plowed through her hair while his mouth whispered over her lips.

"You aren't alone in this, Maggie," he murmured right before he kissed her.

She finally melted against him, giving into the feeling of coming home in his arms. And for a few blissful moments, she forgot that a murder had occurred in her kitchen and the killer was still free.

"You don't mind me horning in on your time with Kenny and Ashley?" Kane clasped Maggie's hand as they walked back toward the apartment building after seeing a Saturday afternoon matinee the following weekend.

"Actually it was nice having you along." As she said that, she realized it was really true.

She enjoyed Kane's company—probably too much. She still felt as though he closed part of himself off to her. Whereas after spending most of the evenings during the workweek with him, looking into Sam Maples' and Phillip Johnson's pasts, Kane knew most of her life story—except what she wasn't free to tell him.

Ahead of Maggie, Kenny made a beeline for the ice-cream parlor along Main Street. "I'm going to have to jog twice as long to work off the two scoops I plan on getting."

"Well, in that case, relish every lick to make it worth the time."

Ashley entered the store slightly behind her brother while Maggie and Kane followed at a more sedate pace. The two children were giving their orders at the counter when Maggie entered. No matter how much time she spent in her siblings' company, it was always bittersweet. She knew it would come to an end because over the past few weeks as she had grown closer to Vicky she also realized she couldn't keep up the pretense. She would need to leave soon and return to St. Louis—which was another reason she shouldn't get too serious with Kane.

"You two find us a table while we order," Kane said to the kids.

"I want two scoops of cookie dough ice cream in a waffle cone," Maggie said to the clerk behind the counter.

"And I'll have a double scoop of chocolate in a regular cone." Kane brushed against her as he positioned himself next to her.

"Somehow I figured that would be your order."

"Are you telling me that I'm predictable?"

"Yes." Maggie took her cone and Kane's while he paid for the treats.

"Okay, how about this for unpredictable? Go with me to the faculty gala. It's in connection with the university's hundredth anniversary."

"On a date?"

"That's usually what it means when a man asks a woman out for the evening."

"Why?"

"Most women don't ask why."

"I'm not most women." *What do you want from me?* Although that question was really what Maggie wanted to ask, she wouldn't.

"I could say I need a date, but that isn't totally true. I've gone to functions alone before. I could say it would be a good time for you to meet Sam Maples and Phillip Johnson. I'd love to get your take on them. But I could find another way to have you meet those two. No, the real reason is that I would like to ask you out. I enjoy being with you. You make me forget…" He clamped his jaw shut as though forcing himself from saying any more. "If you don't want to go, I'll understand. I have to warn you it's formal."

"A long-gown formal?"

Kane nodded. "I've got to dust off my black tuxedo."

Maggie noticed her ice cream melting and quickly took several licks while she tried to calm her racing pulse. A date with Kane. Dangerous to her peace of mind—what peace of mind? She hadn't had any since she'd come to Seven Oaks.

"You've got yourself a date then." She loved a man in a tux, and she knew Kane wouldn't disappoint her in that department.

"Maggie. Uncle Kane," Kenny shouted from across the shop. "What's taking you two so long?"

Every pair of eyes in the ice-cream parlor fixed upon her and Kane, standing only half a foot apart.

"We're coming." Maggie hurried toward the children, hoping her face wasn't as red as it felt.

"Can we have seconds?" Ashley asked when Maggie sat next to her.

"I'm afraid your mother wouldn't be too happy with us if I spoiled your dinner." Maggie scooted over to give Kane more room at the very small round table.

With a pout on her face, Ashley dropped her head for a few seconds.

"In fact, we can't stay too long. It's getting late." Kane ruffled Ashley's hair. "Maybe another time, princess."

Her younger sister lifted her gaze, all evidence of a frown gone. Ashley looked right at Maggie. "And go to the movies?"

"Of course. I love to go to the movies."

"Me, too." Ashley gave Maggie a smile. "Next week?"

"Ashley!" Kenny said in his "adult" voice.

"That's okay, Kenny. Ashley, isn't next weekend filled

with activities centered around Seven Oaks University's Centennial Celebration?" Maggie caught Kane's gaze, thoughts of their upcoming date causing heat to flood her cheeks.

"Oh, yeah, I forgot. Mommy said something about that."

"There's going to be a huge barbecue and fireworks Friday night with lots of activities at the school on Saturday, so I have a feeling you all will be busy." Kane rose. "We'd better get a move on it."

As dusk settled over Seven Oaks, streaks of orange, yellow and rose painted the sky. Maggie strolled next to Kane with the children running ahead toward home.

After depositing Ashley and Kenny in their apartment, Maggie turned to Kane. "I can fix a couple of sandwiches for supper."

"Sure. But maybe I should prepare the food."

"I had my second cooking lesson. I'm not that bad." Maggie unlocked her front door and entered.

"Okay. While you're making the sandwiches, I'll fix the coffee."

Maggie headed toward her kitchen. "I got a new coffeemaker and put Henry's back with his possessions. David and another officer had just finished going through all the boxes."

"Yeah, he called me and told me he didn't find another flash drive."

"There were probably only two." Maggie withdrew the ingredients she needed from the refrigerator, then reached for the utensil drawer.

She stopped and looked at it. Why was it slightly open? "I'm sure I shut this earlier."

Kane glanced at her. "What? The drawer?"

"Yes. It wasn't closed all the way." *I'm being paranoid.* She shrugged. "Right before we left for the movies, I was in hurry. I might have left it open in my haste." She retrieved a knife from the drawer and shut it all the way. "I hate not feeling totally safe. It makes me question everything."

"I'm sorry about that, Maggie." Kane switched the coffee-maker on, then angled toward her. "I wish I could change that. The offer still stands. If at any time you want out of your rental contract, I'll let you at no cost to you."

No! I'm finally getting to know Ashley. Today was the first time I didn't feel like a stranger to my own sister. "I'll be fine. It takes more than an intruder to get to me. I've put this all in the Lord's hands. It'll work out." Maggie busied herself putting the ham and Swiss cheese on the bread, then topping them with tomato slices and lettuce.

"How can you say that with what's happened?"

"Easy. If I didn't believe that, what would I have? Nothing really. God gives me hope. We all need that, especially during the tough times. My faith held me together when my adopted mother rejected me. God doesn't reject—only people."

"When I witnessed a friend die before me, I begged the Lord to make things different. He didn't. The war still raged around me. I still had people I know die or become wounded."

"You're here now. You have a full life. The Lord never guaranteed that life would be easy, but He did guarantee He would be with us every step of the way. Holding us up, making us stronger."

The scent of coffee spiced the air. Maggie cut the sandwiches into halves, then picked up the plates. "Grab two mugs, and come into the living room. We'll eat in there." With the constant reminder of Henry's murder, she was having a hard time staying very long in the kitchen.

Maggie took a seat on the couch and placed the food on the table in front of her. When Kane came into the room, she put two coasters down for the mugs as he sat next to her.

Maggie caught sight of the marble mantel. "I always built

fires in my fireplace every weekend during the winter in St. Louis. This one is beautiful."

"I'll have to come up and enjoy yours. That's the one thing my apartment in the basement doesn't have and I miss."

"Why did you move downstairs?"

"After I was injured and came back to the States to recover, I had trouble climbing stairs. I converted part of the basement area into an apartment and fulfilled a dream of having a workshop. For a while I used the back door in the basement as an entrance."

"So you didn't have a workshop until a few years ago?"

"No. Making furniture became a kind of therapy for me. Still is."

"I'm impressed. You got awfully good in a short amount of time."

"I spend a lot of time in my workshop."

Hiding away from people. She'd spent a lot of time in her room while growing up and later in her apartment doing that very thing. This move forced her to come out of her comfort zone in order to discover what she wanted to know. That didn't mean she didn't get the urge to do what Ashley often did—hide.

"How long did it take you to heal from your injuries?"

Kane stared at the grate in the fireplace across the room. He hadn't healed. But he couldn't say that. Then she would ask him more questions about his injuries. He wasn't ready to open himself up to her pity. He still could remember Ruth's reaction. The first time he'd seen it in her eyes, something died in him that day. So when she left him, he hadn't really been surprised. He'd been a lousy companion.

"It took a few months before I could comfortably use the staircase to the first floor," he finally said, feeling her gaze on him. He reached and picked up his sandwich although his stomach knotted in a tight ball.

"What happened between you and your fiancée? Edwina said she went to your parents' house with you while you recovered, but she came back alone and moved from Seven Oaks right after that."

He'd been so glad Ruth was gone by the time he came back to town. At least he hadn't had to live with the constant reminder that he'd lost more than his leg that fateful day in Iraq. "I'm not the man she fell in love with. She recognized it and put an end to our engagement."

"I'm sorry," Maggie murmured, delving into her own sandwich.

Kane started to say she had nothing to be sorry for, but his throat constricted around the words. *Lay everything out on the table now before you end up hurt again.* The words were there in his mind, but he couldn't get them past his lips.

Finishing her last bite, Maggie wiped her mouth with a napkin, then shifted toward him. "Do you like to jog? I've been looking for a running partner. Come jogging with me tomorrow afternoon."

"I don't jog."

"But you look like you're in shape."

"I go to a gym."

"I promise I'll go slow. It would be fun to have someone to run with."

Kane shot to his feet. "No!" He scooped up his empty plate and marched into the kitchen. At the sink, he washed off the dish and then put it in the drainer.

"I'm sorry."

He spun around. "You have nothing to be sorry about. Not before. Not now." A pressure tightened about his chest. He pulled air into his lungs, but it didn't seem like enough. "I can't run well because of my leg."

"Oh. I'm so—" Maggie attempted a grin that faded instantly. "I shouldn't have pushed."

He covered the space between them. "And I shouldn't have shouted. I used to jog all the time." He combed his fingers through her hair and held her head. "Please accept my apology."

"No problem."

But her hurt leaked through her words and wounded him. He shouldn't be so touchy, but before his injury, he'd always been very athletic and enjoyed doing anything that pushed him physically.

Maggie moved from his touch and put her own plate in the sink. "It's been a long day. We probably should discuss what we should do next about Henry's murder, but I'm just too tired to make sense out of all that's happened. How about tomorrow afternoon?"

"Fine. I should hear back from my friend at Henry's old school. Vince has been away, but his wife said he'll be home late tonight."

"Good. I'd love to know what Henry was like in Nashville."

"I doubt any different."

"Which means he may have made some enemies there?"

"Yep, but I don't think the person who killed Henry lives anywhere but here in Seven Oaks."

Maggie's shoulders sagged. "I was afraid you would say that."

"Are you still afraid someone is looking for something in this apartment?"

"I guess not. But I'll feel better when it's settled."

Kane started for the front door. "Come to the workshop after church tomorrow. We'll talk then."

He paused in the entrance, wanting to drag her into his embrace and kiss her again. He needed to keep his distance.

He wasn't good at relationships. Ruth had made that loud and clear to him when she'd left him.

"Good night, Maggie."

The sound of the door closing reverberated down the hallway. He stood in the corridor, the urge to go back into her apartment and tell her everything so strong that he had to force himself to move toward the stairs.

With her palm flat against the wood of the door, Maggie leaned into it, trying to visualize Kane walking away from her apartment. She'd gotten a glimpse of the hurt that Ruth had wielded by leaving him.

She turned away, heading toward her bedroom. Passing her office, she decided to check her e-mail before going to bed early. Through a doctor she knew at the hospital, she'd discovered the address of the fireman who had been the arson investigator back in the 1970s. She'd contacted him several days ago and hoped he'd answer her about the Johnsons' house fire.

Sitting down at the desk, Maggie breathed deeply, a faint odd odor hanging in the air she couldn't identify. Of course, it hadn't been that long ago she'd been around a lot of people at the movie theater and ice-cream parlor, and this was the first time she'd been alone and quiet enough even to focus on her surroundings.

Glancing down, she noticed the drawer on the left-hand side was slightly open, too. She'd read her messages earlier today and had no reason to get into that drawer. She pulled it toward her and examined its few contents—mostly pens, paper clips and pencils.

As her laptop booted up, she scanned the office and could find nothing else out of place. And if she were truthful with herself, she'd probably left the drawer open.

Since the break-in a few weeks before, she questioned everything to the point she was driving herself crazy. Worry had become her way of life, and she didn't like it. *Lord, I have to learn to turn it over to You. What I can't control is in Your hands.*

When her e-mails appeared up on her screen, she ran down the list and found a response from the retired arson investigator. After reading it, she called Kane.

He answered on the third ring. "Hi. Is everything okay?"

"Yes, the arson investigator I told you I was going to contact e-mailed me back. He now lives in Lexington, and he's willing to meet with us. Are you up for a road trip one afternoon this week? I can get off either Tuesday or Wednesday."

"Wednesday. I'm only working a half day. We can leave after lunch or get lunch on the way to Lexington. It's about an hour away."

"Great. Lunch and a visit with Mr. Preston. Good night." Maggie hung up and immediately typed a reply, setting up an appointment to talk with the arson investigator at three.

Weary, she made her way to her bedroom and quickly dressed for bed, switching on her sound machine she used to drown out noise during the night. She wasn't even going to bother to read because as tired as she was, it wouldn't be long before she was asleep.

EIGHT

An alarm blared. Maggie shot up in bed and stared at the darkness surrounding her, trying to orient herself to the sound still blasting the stillness.

Not my clock.

Then it dawned on Maggie what it was. Her fire alarm!

A pounding at her front door propelled her from bed. Grabbing her robe and donning it, she raced from the room and in the hallway met a wall of smoke pouring from her office.

Maggie spun back into her room and frantically scanned for anything to put over her mouth and nose. Snatching up a T-shirt lying on the chair nearby, she held it to her face and turned back to the hallway. Running low, she headed for her front door.

Suddenly it burst open, and Kane hurried into her apartment, his chest rising and falling rapidly.

He saw her. Relief moved across his features. "I called the fire department. Edwina was up and heard your alarm. She's getting everyone else out of the building. Get out now."

Maggie straightened. "It's coming from my office."

How long had the alarm been going off? Had she slept through some of it?

She shook off the cobwebs of sleep still clinging to her

mind and grabbed Kane's arm as he passed her. "Where are you going? Aren't you leaving, too?"

"In a sec. I may be able to stop the fire." He held up a large fire extinguisher he was carrying.

"Then I'm coming with you."

He thrust his face into hers. "No! Leave now!"

"What if something happens to you?"

"Didn't you tell me to put my trust in the Lord? I'm in His hands." He directed her to the door and gently pushed her out into the hallway.

Pandemonium erupted around Maggie in the corridor. Kyra, in a robe, tugged a sleepy Sean by her while Marcus Quinn cradled Ann to him as he came down the steps from the third floor. Vicky's door opened, and she and the children surged out of the apartment.

Maggie sent a prayer of thanks to the Lord as she took Kenny's hand and started for the staircase.

"Where's Uncle Kane?" the boy asked, glancing back toward Maggie's place.

"Good question." Halfway down the steps, Maggie checked to see if everyone in the building was heading out the main entrance. They were—except for Kane.

She released her grip on Kenny, and over the noise of confused voices and children crying, she said to Vicky, "I'm going to drag Kane out of here. I'll be out in a minute."

"Don't. He can take care of himself." Dropping Ashley's hand for a second, Vicky grasped Maggie's arms to stop her going back up the stairs.

The idea that Vicky cared about her now stirred the anger Maggie had managed to suppress lately. It was too late. Pushing the feeling aside, she concentrated on the here and now. "I'll be fine. I've been taking care of myself for years."

Maggie jerked free at the same time Ashley's eyes widened

and her hand went to her mouth. "Rosie is still in the apartment. I've got to get her."

"No, you can't." Vicky grabbed for her youngest.

But Ashley was already running up the stairs. Vicky started after her.

Maggie blocked her. "I'll get her and send her back down. Go. Make sure Kenny gets out all right. Where's John?"

"Studying at the library. It was too noisy in our apartment."

Maggie whirled around and raced back up the staircase to the second floor. She wasn't going to let anything happen to her kid sister. She couldn't lose her.

Inside Vicky's place, she scanned the area and decided to head for Ashley and Kenny's room. Near the hall the little girl rushed out of her bedroom, holding the snake that her brother had brought home from school.

"You've got to get out of here." Maggie scooped Ashley into her arms and rushed toward the hallway and safety.

The scent of smoke assailed her nostrils. Maggie quickened her steps. At the top of the stairs, she put Ashley down as Vicky climbed the steps two at a time.

"Go to your mom." Then to Vicky, Maggie asked, "Did Kane come down yet?"

"No." Her birth mother snatched Ashley up into her arms and hurried down the stairs.

In the distance the sirens wailed as Maggie reentered her apartment and called out, "Kane!"

Each second she didn't see or hear him heightened her panic that the smoke had gotten to him. Through the haze, Maggie started for her office, holding the T-shirt over her mouth again.

How am I going to drag Kane from my apartment if he passed out? This ran through her mind as she searched her smoky surroundings.

His eyes watering, Kane popped his head out of the doorway. "I think I've taken care of the fire. I think it started in the trash can by the desk. Thankfully I came when I did. The drapes had caught fire. This whole place could have gone up." Coughing, he gripped her arm and rushed toward the corridor. "Let's get out of here and let the firemen do their job."

Started in the trash can? How?

Sweat coated her face, her eyes were stinging, too, from the smoke. Coughing racked her as well as she raced down the stairs. Fires have been known to restart from just one spark. She prayed Kane had completely put it out.

When Maggie emerged from the building, the tenants stood by the street. The firefighters scrambled from the fire engine when it came to a stop. A quick scan confirmed everyone was accounted for, and Maggie sagged against Kane in relief.

"What am I going to do?" Maggie asked, sitting in Edwina's apartment later that night. "My place reeks of smoke, and the office will have to be completely redone. I guess I can move back to the dormitory for the time being."

"Nonsense. You can stay here. I have an extra bedroom for when my grandnieces and nephews come to visit. I'm just glad Kane put it out when he did and that each apartment's ventilation system is separate."

"Yeah, at least no one else in the building will have to find another place to live."

A knock sounded at the door.

"I'll get it for you." Maggie rose and let Kane into the apartment. "What else did the fire department say?" She remembered seeing him talking to the fire chief when she'd trudged back into the building.

"They've inspected the office and determined the fire started in the trash can."

"I don't see how." She raked her fingers through her hair then massaged her nape, trying to ease the tension radiating down her spine and across her shoulders.

"From a cigarette." Limping toward the couch, Kane collapsed on it and rubbed his left knee, pain etched into his features.

"Are you all right? Did you hurt yourself?" Maggie asked, taking the seat next to him.

"Just overdid it tonight, but at least everyone is safe."

"Kane, I don't smoke. How did a cigarette get into my trash can?"

"Good question. Has anyone been in the apartment today who was smoking? They can smolder a while before causing a fire." Kane shifted toward Maggie.

"No one has been in there for the past few days but you and Edwina." She remembered the two drawers slightly open. Maybe she hadn't been paranoid after all. "What if my intruder is back looking for something?"

Edwina struggled to her feet, tired lines emphasizing her wrinkles. "How did he get in with the new security system?"

"Where there's a will, there's a way. Or he lives in the building." Icy fingers gripped Maggie in a vise. She hugged her arms to her chest. She'd wondered about that after the first break-in; then she had dismissed it as she'd gotten to know the other tenants.

"But still he has to get into your place somehow once he's in the building." Edwina plodded toward her kitchen and reappeared a minute later. "Here's my set of keys for each apartment. I keep it hidden if I don't have them with me."

Kane dug into his pocket and withdrew his set. "And here's mine. It's always with me."

"I don't know how someone got in, but he did and he started that fire either deliberately or accidentally. Either way I'm without a home for at least a while. Maybe that was his purpose. To get me out of the apartment." Head throbbing, Maggie clenched her hands. "He doesn't know me very well. I won't be scared away."

"Nor does he know me. I made a promise to you, and I intend to keep it. We'll just need to step up our search for the murderer. Once found, your problems will be over with." Kane patted Maggie's fist lying on the couch between them.

She wished her problems would be over when that happened, but she still had the situation with Vicky and her family. Finding the killer might be easier than dealing with her past and her fear of rejection.

Kane struggled to his feet, leaning heavily on his right leg. "I'll get someone out here to look at your apartment first thing tomorrow—" he glanced at his watch "—this morning. At least the fire was confined to your place. Where are you going to stay until then?"

"Right here in my spare bedroom," Edwina said as she shuffled toward her short hallway. "I'm going to put fresh sheets on the bed right now."

"I can help—"

"Maggie, nonsense. You're my guest. I'll take care of it." Edwina peered back at her, winked, then continued to amble down the hall.

Maggie chuckled. "Can you believe in the middle of all that's going on she's trying to play matchmaker?"

"Edwina never changes. She's always been like that, and I've known her since I was a child. I used to go over to visit her with David. She had treats for us and interesting stories about what was going on at the university." Kane turned too quickly toward the front door, throwing his body out of position.

Maggie's arms shot out to steady him before he went down. Anger lined his face, and he wrenched from her embrace, clutching the back of the sofa to keep himself upright.

"I don't need your help. I'm just tired and lost my footing."

"I know that. What's going on, Kane? Maybe the smoke got to you more than you let on with the firefighters."

Limping toward the door, he thrust it open. Keeping his back to her, he said, "Nothing. Everything's wonderful."

Something's wrong. Did he hurt himself while trying to put out the fire? Maggie stared at Kane's retreating figure. The door closing—a bit loudly—shook her out of her trance.

"Kane's left already?" Edwina asked, coming back into the living room.

"Yeah, but he's acting strangely. He's never limped so heavily before. Do you think he hurt himself and doesn't want to let anyone know? My father used to suffer silently when he was in pain."

"Kane's definitely the strong, silent type, and that doesn't stop when it comes to being hurt. Go find out what's wrong."

"I don't know. He's so good at putting up barriers."

"Right and it's about time someone challenged those barriers. He's lived in the past long enough. I can tell he really likes you. You might be able to get through to him. I've tried and haven't been successful."

"What happened to him in the war?"

Edwina frowned. "Make him tell you. It's his story, not mine."

Maggie hurried from Edwina's. She owed Kane and wanted to be there for him if he was hurting physically or emotionally. As much as some people wished they could go through life not needing anyone, it wasn't possible. She was still learning that lesson. When everything settled down, she needed to take a good hard look at her own life and rethink what she was going to do about Vicky and her family. She wanted them in her life. She'd discovered that tonight when she was afraid she might lose Ashley.

She rapped on his door. Nothing, not a sound. Again she knocked, this time pounding. "Kane! Open up."

What if he'd been in more pain than he had let on? Although he'd been checked and breathed in some oxygen the firefighters had, maybe the smoke had done some kind of damage and—

The door flew open, and Kane filled the entranceway with his large presence. Her gaze took in his pain-carved facial features then skimmed down his length. It stopped at the sight of the crutch he was leaning on before continuing its trek to his left leg, missing below the knee. She'd never seen him in shorts before, but now it was evident why.

Her attention riveted to his face. "Is this what you've been hiding all this time from me?"

With a grimace, he nodded. "I guess you want to come in."

Maggie didn't say anything. She was still trying to wrap her mind around what she'd seen and the implications his silence had on their relation—no, correction friendship. Kane not trusting her with the fact he wore a prosthetic leg underscored what little he thought of her. Hurt and anger warred for dominance.

"I didn't tell you about my leg because I don't want your pity." He stepped to the side to let her into his apartment.

She remained in the hallway, anger winning. "Now I know what you really think of me, and it isn't flattering. You think I'm some shallow person who can't accept people for who they are." She poked him in the chest. "Well, buster, I've got news for you. I work at a hospital and work with all kinds of patients. I've actually had a few who've lost a limb and had to learn to deal with it, as well as regain their speech abilities. I never thought any less of them." Whirling around, she started to storm away.

"I'm sorry, Maggie."

His words halted her escape. She turned back, her heart twisting at the chastened look on his face.

"You're right. I prejudged you because of my past experiences with some people. When I came back to Seven Oaks, I was determined not to give anyone around me the chance to pity me or think I couldn't be the man I once was." He swept his arm across his body. "Come in. I owe you an explanation if you'll listen to it now."

Indecision stayed her for all of about ten seconds. She stalked past Kane and swung around in the middle of his living room. With her arms folded over her chest, she watched him maneuver quite well using his one crutch.

"Have a seat. This may take a while." Kane eased into a chair across from his couch. "Does Edwina know where you are? I don't want her to worry."

"Who do you think suggested I come talk to you?"

"Edwina. She's been hounding me to tell you from the beginning."

"Who knows about your leg?"

"A few—John, Vicky, David, Edwina. I made them promise not to speak of it to anyone, even me."

"Not Ashley and Kenny?"

He shook his head.

"Why not?"

He shrugged. "It's not something I like to talk about, and I certainly don't go around announcing it to people."

"You're not less a person because you don't have part of your leg. Do you think you are?"

"Whoa. You don't beat around the bush." He averted his gaze for a long moment. "Right after it happened I had some people, my parents and Ruth included, who made me feel like an invalid, like I would have to change my life because I lost my leg. I've had a hard time accepting what it's done to my life."

"What's it done to you?"

"I used to love to run, participate in all kinds of sports. I was training for a marathon when I was called up. Now I have to be satisfied working out at the gym."

"You can still run. You just need to get a different kind of prosthetic leg. I'd love to have someone to run with and challenge me to go faster and longer. Any time you're up for it, just let me know."

"It's not that easy."

"Yes, it is after you get the prosthesis. You adjust to it and start running. Unless you want to wallow some more in self-pity."

He blinked, his cheeks reddening.

"That's not you. Since when do you let something get you down for long? Ruth wasn't the woman for you. No one is perfect. We all have limitations. I can't sing. I love to sing, but I only sing when I'm alone. But I do sing."

"This isn't anything like singing!"

"Yes, it is. It's a limitation. That's all. Again we all have them. The key is to work around them and not let them stop us from doing what we love to do. So what's it gonna be? Are you going to continue to hide from life or begin living it to the fullest? Our attitude is everything."

Doubt still appeared on Kane's face, his eyes half-veiled.

"Jesus knew His earthly life would be for only a short time, but in that time he did everything he could. He lived it to the fullest and got His message out to the people He'd come to offer salvation to. Look at what he accomplished in such a short time."

"Where's God in war?"

"By your side. He hasn't forsaken you. Wasn't it better for you to discover the kind of person Ruth was before you two got married because marriage is forever—" she gave him a half grin "—or it should be. For better or worse. It looks like she couldn't take the worse."

Kane sank back against the cushion, closing his eyes. Weariness took hold of him, but there was no more doubt in his expression. "Has anyone told you that you'd make a great drill sergeant?"

"Not lately. But some of my patients know I don't give up easily."

"And you think I have?" His gaze fastened onto hers.

"I wouldn't go as far as to say you let the loss of your leg cause you to give up. Rather I think you've retreated from life. Have you thought about going to a support group?"

"I had therapy when this all first happened." He cocked a grin. "And you can see how much good it did."

"Maybe you weren't ready to listen."

"Perhaps." He leaned forward, elbows on the arms of the chair while he steepled his fingers. "You've given me something to think about. I probably shouldn't make any decisions while my brain is mush, though. Besides, my problems aren't the most pressing ones at the moment. We need to talk about what we should do next."

We. She resisted the lure of that word. It didn't mean they were a couple. His silence about his injury proved that to her. "Yes, but let's talk tomorrow after church or rather later today. I can't believe it's four." Maggie rose. "I need to let you get some rest while I go to Edwina's and collapse from exhaustion."

"What time are you going to church?"

"I'm going to the late service. I'll leave about ten-thirty."

"I'd like to go with you."

"You don't have to. Nothing's gonna happen to me at church."

"I know. I just thought I would go with you. Is that okay?"

Very. "Yes." He started to get up. She put her hand up. "Stay. I think I know the way out."

In the hall Maggie couldn't contain her broad smile any longer. In the midst of all that had happened in the last few hours, there was a bright spot. Kane had been looking out for her lately, and now she felt she had returned the favor.

Thank you, Lord.

"This is so beautiful. With all the commotion lately, I haven't had the chance to explore your backyard and the lake." Maggie sat on a wooden bench that faced the water where ducks and Canada geese swam.

"I thought we would get away from the house to do some brainstorming." Kane took the place right next to her, relaxing and slipping his arm along the back. "I got a chance to talk to David at church about the fire. He's going to talk with the arson expert for the fire department. See if there's any kind of evidence to link it to someone."

"I know that arson can be hard to prove. A lot of cases go unsolved or at least not to trial. Look at Phillip Johnson's parents and what happened there."

"Yeah, David said the case is still open. No one was brought in. Too bad the detective on that case is dead. I would love to talk to him about what he suspected. There wasn't anything in the official file to point to anyone, but they sometimes have hunches they just can't prove."

"Hopefully the retired arson investigator will have a suspect when we see him this week. As you said, having a suspect and proving it in court are two different things." His hand rested on her shoulder, and the feeling it generated zipped through her.

"What about your friend at the university in Nashville? Have you heard back from him?"

"Yes. In fact, he woke me up this morning."

"What did he have to say concerning Henry? Any enemies there?"

"Several. Henry left right before an accusation was going

to be brought against him for sexual harassment of a female student. I got the feeling after Henry was gone the university persuaded the young woman not to pursue it in court."

"Bad publicity for the school?"

"Yes. Parents don't want to send their daughters off to a university with a reputation of having a professor who wanted certain sexual favors for a grade."

"The more I hear about this man, the more I don't like him—and I didn't even know him." Maggie tried to picture Henry, and all she saw was a black screen. Like the man's heart?

"I did and we had a few complaints against him from the students, but nothing quite that serious."

"What I want to know is how did he get hired at a prestigious university such as Seven Oaks with that kind of reputation? Isn't that just asking for trouble?"

"I guess that's a question for Dr. Johnson since he was the one who hired him and made him head of the science department."

"Was he at the other school?"

"No, but Henry did have good credentials. His reputation as a scholar was excellent. I suppose since Phillip and Henry were friends not many questions were asked about anything else."

"Or the answers were overlooked. Could Henry have been blackmailing Dr. Johnson?"

NINE

"And blackmailing Dr. Maples, too?" Kane shook his head. "I don't know. I never thought Henry was wanting for money, but now that I think about it, where did the money he have come from?"

"If he was financially well off, why was he living in one of your apartments? Don't get me wrong. You have a very nice building, but why wouldn't he buy a house or live in those deluxe condos on Memorial."

"I'll try not to take offense," Kane said with a grin. "And the answer again is I don't know." Drawing Maggie against him, he lazily ran his hand up and down her arm. "I did get the impression he didn't want the responsibility of keeping up a house. He couldn't be bothered by such mundane activities."

The word *home* and Henry didn't go together from all Maggie had learned about the man. Home was a refuge from the world, a place full of comfort and in the best circumstances, love. She wanted a home and someone to love.

"But again who knows what was going on in Henry's mind." Kane continued to hold her pressed to his side.

Trying to ignore his touch, which definitely distracted her from thinking logically, Maggie asked, "Okay, what do we have? Two flash drives with information on them. The photos could be damaging to Dr. Maples' marriage and career while on Dr. Johnson's we have a story about the death of his parents and childhood photos of the two of them together. Henry could have been keeping the newspaper article because he was mentioned in it. It wouldn't surprise me he was vain on top of everything else."

"Or he could be keeping it because he has something on his friend, Phillip Johnson."

"Then where is that information? Do you see the head of the university killing his mother and father and then covering it up? This is a thirteen-year-old we're talking about." She turned slightly to look into Kane's eyes. "And what do these flash drives have to do with the break-ins at my apartment? David has interviewed both Dr. Maples and Dr. Johnson about Henry. He's checked out their alibis, too."

"Which neither man really has since they both claimed to be asleep when Henry was murdered."

"And their wives say they were. Of course, if someone suspected me of murder at that time of night, I'm usually asleep, and there would be no one to give me an alibi."

"But how reliable is a wife as an alibi? David isn't totally convinced. I know my friend well."

"I think David suspects everyone at this time."

"He's probably ruled out Edwina."

"She has the expertise to pull off a murder. Have you seen her bookshelves? I don't think there's a mystery book she hasn't read." His hand cupping her to him caressed a leisurely path up and down her arm that caused her skin to tingle where he touched her.

"So we're not exactly at square one but close."

Completely relaxing in the shelter of his embrace, she tilted her head back to peer up at him. He combed her hair away from her face, hooking some strands behind her ear.

Tenderness glittered in his eyes. The sensation of being cherished flowed through Maggie, and she didn't want to move. She wanted to capture this moment forever.

A goose nearby honked, startling her. She gasped and stiffened at the harsh sound.

"Relax. At least for a few minutes." He drew her back into the curve of his arm.

But reality had already returned. What was she doing? Kane still had huge hurdles to overcome and wasn't any more ready to get serious about anyone. Just like her. Both of their lives were in turmoil. Adding the complications of a relationship didn't make sense to her.

"Who else at the university might hold a grudge against Henry?" she asked to get them back on track.

"It's not a short list. There's Thomas Sellman. At the end of last year, Henry messed up his chances for a scholarship. Thomas had to take out a loan to finish his master's. We've talked about Beth dating Henry when he first came here. It didn't end well. Most of the professors in his department loathe him. He's made their lives miserable these past two years. Several of his secretaries have left in a huff, declaring he's too demanding and disrespectful. The latest mentioned she was having problems and was looking for another position at the university."

"Kyra Williams who lives upstairs?" She was so quiet and nice, also a wonderful mother from what Maggie could see when the woman was with her son.

Kane nodded.

"Okay, I get the picture. No wonder David looks so tired. This investigation must be running him around in circles, especially since the university is putting pressure on him to solve it fast. Did Henry do anything good?"

"I didn't think so until Edwina told me about the Southside Recreational Center. I'm sure his support will be missed."

"That's right. She told me that. Anything else?" Maggie finally let the tension go and totally relaxed against Kane again.

"He was a great fund-raiser for the university. Some of the wealthy alumni gave large sums of money after Henry persuaded them. I have a feeling the board of trustees was happy about that."

"Maybe that's why Dr. Johnson hired Henry."

"It's a possibility. This next weekend at the festivities maybe we'll get a chance to corner our president when he doesn't expect it." Kane framed her face between his palms. "Now let's move on to something more—interesting."

Suddenly the day turned very warm. A lump formed in her throat as his eyelids slid down to veil the glint in his gaze. He feathered his mouth across hers, then laid claim to it in a kiss that rocked her to her toes.

When he parted, he laid his forehead against hers, his hands still cupping her. "I think you should leave this apartment."

His statement threw her off-kilter after that dynamite kiss. She pulled back. "No! This is my home, and no one is going to run me off."

"Don't be ridiculous. You could have died last night."

"I don't think the fire was started deliberately."

"How can you say that? You don't know for sure."

Because she was desperate to believe it was true. No one was targeting her personally. No one wanted her dead like Henry. "Someone is after something he believes is in my apartment. If we find it first, then everything will be back to normal again."

"Normal! There's nothing about murder that's normal." Kane stood, hovering over her with his hands balled at his sides.

"Help me search my place. There were two flash drives. Maybe there's another one hidden somewhere. What's on the first drives isn't what the intruder is after?"

"We don't know that for sure either. David hasn't gone

around advertising the information on them. Maybe your attacker doesn't know we found them."

She rose, putting some space between them. "I'm going to spend this afternoon going through my apartment until I'm satisfied there's nothing else there."

"The police already did."

"But we still found two since they did."

Kane threw his hands up in the air. "Fine. I'll help. Maybe we should rip the furniture apart to see if he managed to hide something in one of the pieces."

"It's possible, but there's no way you should destroy your beautiful pieces to search. We'll have to find another way to check the furniture."

"I was kidding, Maggie." A smile broke through his neutral expression.

"I knew that."

"No, you didn't."

"Okay, I admit that I'm a tad bit focused on this."

His laughter vied with the sounds of the fussing geese across the pond. "Only a tad. I'd hate to see you when you're totally focused." He took her hand. "Let's go 'drive' hunting."

"It could be something other than a flash drive."

"Let's not muddy the water just yet."

After an uneventful few days, Kane turned onto the street in Lexington on Wednesday afternoon to visit the retired arson investigator. "I hope he has a lead for us."

"If he doesn't, confronting Dr. Maples and Dr. Johnson at the gala Saturday is about all we have left." Maggie brushed her hair behind her ear, something he noticed she did when she was nervous or worried.

"It's getting to you."

"What do you mean?" She didn't look at him.

"Sunday you were hoping we'd find another flash drive that would give David the killer. We didn't. On top of that, you have to live out of a suitcase in someone else's apartment. You've had to throw away quite a few of your possessions because of the fire. I don't think you've been sleeping well."

"So much for hiding the bags under my eyes with makeup. I probably get about three hours of sleep a night. Anyone involved in this affair who smokes? We never discussed that."

"I've seen Phillip Johnson and Thomas Sellman. There may be more—probably is. But if the police brought in everyone who smokes, they would have their hands full."

"How about smokes and hates Henry?"

"What if it isn't obvious the person hates Henry?" Kane parked his car.

"Good point. People put up facades all the time."

Like him. His walls around his heart were so high it would be difficult to climb over. He'd been so busy running from his past he'd forgotten the direction he was headed. Maybe that was his problem—he really didn't have a direction. Was his reason for quitting his job at the university because he could then hide in his workshop and only come out occasionally for human companionship?

He could lose himself for hours making a piece of furniture, but perhaps in that process he had lost himself completely. Had he used Ruth's desertion as an excuse to quit living?

"Kane, are you all right?"

He blinked, focusing on Maggie's worried expression. "What did you say?"

"You seemed lost in thought."

Lost is definitely the right word to describe me. Is it too late to find my way back home, Lord? Do you have room in Your heart to forgive me for turning away? "I was just thinking about my job at the school."

"Having second thoughts of retiring at the age of thirty-four?"

He chuckled. "I think you're mocking me."

"Who me?" She splayed her hand over her heart. "I would never do that. Let's get this interview over with."

A minute later Kane and Maggie rang the bell and waited on the porch. "I know of a great little restaurant in Lexington we can eat an early dinner at on the way back to Seven Oaks."

"I'll need to get back for my Wednesday night cooking lesson."

When Gil Preston answered, he welcomed both of them with a handshake. "I've been looking over my notes on the Johnson fire to refresh my memory. It isn't what it used to be." Maneuvering a cane, he guided them toward his den where he gestured they take a seat on the couch. After easing into a lounge chair, he continued, "When I e-mailed you, Ms. Ridgeway, I hadn't remembered this, but a few years back someone else came to see me about that fire."

Kane gripped Maggie's hand and squeezed gently. "Who?"

"Let me see. What was his name?" The older man scratched his head. "I seem to remember he was tied to the case somehow. I'm awful with names. If I hadn't written yours down, I wouldn't have remembered who was coming to see me."

Maggie leaned forward. "Do you remember what he looked like? Anything about him?"

"He was a big man—not fat, but tall, broad shoulders."

"Young or old?"

"At my age the term *young man* is relative, but I would guess he was in his early forties. He had dark brown hair and he wore wire-rimmed glasses. Not too friendly really. His name was…" The retired arson investigator rubbed a hand across his forehead.

"Henry Payne," Kane said because the description fit Henry down to the glasses.

"Yes, I think so. Do you know him?"

Kane nodded. "He was killed last month. What did you tell him?"

"Not much he didn't already know from the newspaper accounts. Except at first I didn't think it was a deliberate act of arson."

"Why?" Maggie's hold on Kane's hand strengthened, tension pouring off her.

"The accelerant found in the basement was alcohol. At first I thought it might be because someone dropped a bottle that somehow caught on fire. But I determined quickly enough there were at least three or four bottles on that floor—too much for just one. Later the coroner told me about the sleeping pills in both Dr. and Mrs. Johnson."

"Enough to knock them out?" Kane slid a glance toward Maggie, who had gone still. None of the newspaper articles had talked about the sleeping pills.

"No, but they had been drinking, and the combination could have put them out, so they wouldn't have awakened easily when the house was on fire."

"Is it possible that they caused the mess in the basement, went up to bed and never woke up?" Kane asked.

"Possibly, but the pattern I discerned was one of rage, not accidental, as if someone had thrown liquor bottles against the floor and walls in a fit of anger."

"What did Henry do after you told him?" Maggie shivered against him.

"He was very somber, but he thanked me and left after I went through what I knew about the case."

"Can you think of anything else? Something you didn't think of when Henry came to visit you?" Kane fished into his pocket for his business card.

Gil shook his head. "No. I was sorry I could never close that case, but it wasn't the only one that went unsolved. That poor child was left without a home. I remember that Henry's aunt let the Johnson boy stay with them for a while until a family member could be found. I believe he left Seven Oaks after that."

Kane rose and handed the older man his card. "If you think of anything else, please call."

Mr. Preston slid the card into his shirt pocket and stood, walking them to the door. "You know there was one thing you might be interested in. The fact the accelerant was liquor wasn't disclosed at the time to the press. I told Mr. Payne about that, and he got excited for a moment."

As he and Maggie left Gil Preston's house, Kane said, "What do you think about what he told us?"

"I'm not sure. That seems to be the state of mind I've been in lately."

Join the club, Kane thought and opened the car door for Maggie. As he rounded the front of the vehicle, he remembered what the minister at Maggie's church had talked about the past Sunday. The prodigal son was always welcomed back into the fold. Maybe he should check into the support group he'd quit a few months after he had returned to Seven Oaks. Perhaps they still met once a week.

Friday night, the wool blanket beneath Maggie warded off the chill of the evening now that the sun had set. Sitting pressed up against Kane also helped.

"When are the fireworks gonna start? The sun's gone. Why aren't they starting?" Ashley's excited voice floated to Maggie. The child leaned around Kane and added, "The red and green ones are the bestest."

"I like the gold ones. When they go off, it's like stars are raining down on us." Maggie took a deep breath of the smell of freshly mowed grass.

"Where's Mom and Dad? They should be here by now." Kenny squirmed on the blanket spread over the ground.

As Maggie scanned all the stately buildings, some a hundred years old, that surrounded the large commons area in the center of Seven Oaks University, she looked for Vicky and John. "They'll be here as soon as they can."

"Mommy's been gone a lot this week." Ashley stuck her thumb into her mouth.

"Your mom is the secretary to the president and has certain details she needs to attend to involving this anniversary party for the university. This is an important occasion for the school." Their relationship had improved, but Maggie still couldn't hug Ashley when she was hurting.

"I'm important, too."

Even in the growing darkness, Maggie saw the pout tugging at the little girl's mouth. "You're very important."

"They're coming," Kenny shouted, pointing to a couple strolling across the green.

"The party can begin." Kane captured Maggie's gaze and held it while Vicky and John approached and sat on the edge of the blanket.

Ashley took her thumb out of her mouth. "What took you so long, Mommy?"

"Dr. Johnson wanted me to check on the guys who were setting off the fireworks. It should start in a few minutes. They were finishing up when I left."

"Do you enjoy working for Dr. Johnson?" Maggie asked, realizing in all the time she had spent with Vicky they had never talked about her birth mother's work.

"It's a job," Vicky said with a lift of her shoulders. "I'd rather be home with the children." The last sentence was added in a whisper while Kane and John talked quietly. "It should calm down after this weekend celebration, but I guess it won't totally until the police solve Henry's murder. It keeps the school in the spotlight, and Dr. Johnson has to field questions he isn't pleased about."

"I imagine he has," Maggie said, thinking about what she had discovered on the flash drive.

Vicky leaned even closer, keeping an eye on her two children. "David came to see him recently, and after that Dr. Johnson was a bear. I think David was there about the murder. Maybe he was telling Dr. Johnson there was no prime suspect and the case wasn't going well. I did hear my boss tell David to keep him informed of what was going on with the investigation so he could do damage control where the university is concerned."

Dr. Johnson had lost both parents when he was a young teen. That had to be hard on him, and now David's questions probably had brought all those memories back.

"They're starting." Kenny stared at the sky above the Seven Oaks Administration Building.

Ashley moved over to her mother and sat partially in her lap. "Ohh, that's beautiful."

Different colors from red to silver burst open and drizzled toward the ground. The darkness was lit with the display.

Kane scooted next to Maggie and cradled her against him. "John was telling me about the ranting and raving Phillip was doing at the staging area of the fireworks. According to some of the behind-the-scenes workers, he's been extra demanding and not pleased with anything being done."

"I wonder if David's little visit upset the man. Vicky said he was hard to be around after David left."

"Stirring up bad memories can do that to a person."

There was a wealth of meaning in Kane's words that went beyond Dr. Johnson's reaction to David's visit. Maggie slanted a look toward Kane. His features were set in hard lines.

"I've discovered you can't run from those bad memories. They'll go wherever you go until you deal with them."

"Yeah, I know." He fell silent for the rest of the fireworks although his arm stayed around her, holding her close.

Later as she and Kane with the Penningtons in the lead walked back toward Twin Oaks Apartments, he took her hand and whispered into her ear, "I went to my support group yesterday evening."

The revelation thrilled her. "And?"

"I'm going back next Thursday. You're right. I can't keep running. I need to make a stand and deal with my problems about losing my leg, about Ruth."

She grinned. "Haven't I told you I'm always right?"

"I'll keep that in mind when you give me more of that sage advice," he said with a chuckle.

At the house the Penningtons said good-night and headed inside while Kane trapped her on the porch with his arms shackling her back against him.

When silence finally ruled, his breath fanned her neck right before he said, "Don't forget about the gala tomorrow night."

"Vicky and I are going shopping tomorrow. She wants to help me pick out a gown."

"Isn't that cutting it a little close?"

"When she heard I was going with you and didn't have a long gown, she insisted she go with me. She wants to live vicariously through me since she says she has to wear the same gown she's had for years. I couldn't say no, and she couldn't go until tomorrow when all her duties involving the centennial celebration are finished as far as the planning goes." *Almost like a mother and daughter.* The thought saddened Maggie because she'd never really had that with her adoptive mother.

"You two are becoming good friends."

Maggie did her best not to tense in his embrace, but she didn't quite disguise the effect of his last sentence.

"What's wrong?" He kissed her neck below her ear, then kneaded his hands along her shoulders.

"I think everything is catching up with me." Which was true because Kane's observation was right. She liked Vicky. In another life she could have been the woman's good friend. *How can I now, though? Maybe I need to take Kane up on his offer to move from the apartment building at least.*

Kane turned her to face him. "I know what you mean. It's been a long week and an even longer weekend."

He lowered his mouth to hers and for a moment she forgot everything but being with a man she cared about. A man she'd tried not to become emotionally involved with but she was— deeply. His pain was becoming hers. That revelation scared her. It was likely she needed to leave not just the apartment building but Seven Oaks, because although Kane was taking steps to change, she wasn't sure he could totally forgive and forget what had happened to him. She also knew she couldn't tell him about Vicky being her mother, and there was no way she would have a long-term relationship with him and keep that kind of secret from him.

"I enjoyed tonight. I'd forgotten what it was like to go on a date." He hooked his arm around her and walked her to Edwina's place.

Yes, dating. She shouldn't have started because now she would have a hard time backing away from him. And long-distance relationships didn't work. She'd known several friends who had tried them, and they'd all ended with each person going in separate directions.

"Thanks." She stood on tiptoe and gave him a quick kiss. "I enjoyed tonight, too. See you tomorrow." Maggie let herself into the apartment.

Edwina hadn't gone to the fireworks but insisted on watching them from the backyard. She must already be asleep.

As Maggie made her way toward her bedroom, she noticed a note taped to her door. "A Mr. Alexander from Nashville called while you were out. He would like you to call him on Monday at 615-555-2376. It's important he talk to you then."

Maggie snatched the note down and moved into the room. Sitting on the bed, she pulled out her cell, turned it on and saw a message from Mr. Alexander on it, too. He'd called both her cell and home, which she'd forwarded to Edwina's while she stayed with her. Maybe she shouldn't have turned off her cell phone, but she'd drawn the line at having it on during her date with Kane. She hadn't wanted to be disturbed for even a minute.

Now her curiosity would bug her the whole weekend. Who was Mr. Alexander? Why did he want to talk to her?

Maybe she could still reach him. Maggie punched in his number.

A woman's voice, obviously a recording, came on and said, "You have reached the law firm of Alexander and Cussler. The offices are closed until eight on Monday morning."

Maggie hung up. Mr. Alexander was a lawyer. The same questions still nagged her, and she wasn't going to get any answers until Monday morning.

TEN

"**I**'m going to suggest to your president you all have some kind of gala event once a month. It isn't every day a gal gets to see a man in a monkey suit. You don't look half bad, mister."

Kane arched an eyebrow at Maggie as he took her arm to lead her into the ballroom at the luxury hotel in Seven Oaks. "You and Vicky didn't do so bad yourself."

Maggie looked away, not wanting him to read the war waging inside her. When she'd forgotten who Vicky was, she'd really enjoyed shopping with her. She still had no answer concerning what to do about the dilemma developing in her over her birth mother and other family.

"This place is beautiful. I love art deco. When was the hotel built?" Maggie pushed thoughts of the reason she was in Seven Oaks into the background and surveyed the large room before her.

"In 1928. Not long after it was completed, the man who built it went bankrupt. The Great Depression had caught up with him. A company in the early 1990s bought the hotel and restored it to its former glory."

Four massive chandeliers offered illumination, a golden glow radiating from them that enriched the surroundings. A colorful, geometric pattern spread across the arched ceiling.

Snowy white linen tablecloths, arrangements of white roses, crystal and white and gold china lent elegance to the festivities.

"I feel like I stepped into a fairy tale."

Kane looked around. "This place does that to people."

"The university went all out for this celebration."

"I think Dr. Johnson upped the stakes after Henry was murdered. He wanted to counter the negative press we've received this past six weeks."

"If this doesn't do it, nothing will." Maggie walked beside Kane toward the front of the room near the band and dance floor.

"I've arranged for us to sit at Dr. Johnson's table."

"I'll finally get to meet the man. I've heard some interesting things about him."

Kane leaned toward her. "Play nice. We don't really know anything."

"I'll try." She sent him a saucy smile.

When she and Kane arrived, there were two places left at the table—next to the president. Kane pulled back the chair beside Phillip Johnson and seated her. The older gentleman sitting to her left shifted around to greet her.

"Kane told me he would be bringing a date. Then I discovered you live right across the hall from my secretary. Vicky has spoken highly of you. I'm Dr. Phillip Johnson. It's a pleasure to meet you." He held out his hand.

Maggie fit hers within his, his touch damp. "I'm Maggie Ridgeway. You put on quite a party."

"We only turn one hundred once."

"True. The university's association with Seven Oaks Hospital was one of the things that drew me to Seven Oaks to work. The school is well-respected, especially in the medical and science areas."

A tic in his thin face twitched. His gaze hardened for a few seconds before a wide grin spread across his face. "With all that's happened, I hope our reputation hasn't been damaged."

"I'm sure it will survive. Your staff is stellar. Just last week I read Dr. Payne's latest article on biogenesis. Excellent. Too bad about what happened to him."

"You work at Seven Oaks Hospital?"

"I'm a speech therapist and spend a lot of time there. But to tell you the truth, I have a great interest in science. I almost majored in biochemistry."

"That's the scientific world's loss." Dr. Johnson looked beyond her to Kane. "We have a few important contributors here tonight. I hope you'll spend some time appeasing their fears, Kane."

Tension radiated off the president the more she had talked about science. When she'd actually mentioned Dr. Payne, his jaw had clenched, and she'd noticed his hand next to her had balled.

"I'll talk to them. The police are closing in on who did it." Kane took a sip of his ice water, sliding his gaze toward Maggie.

Dr. Johnson's eyes widened. "I hadn't heard that."

"I can tell that David is getting excited about a couple of leads he's gotten lately."

"What are the leads?"

"He's closedmouthed about them. But we've been friends since childhood, and I can read him well. It comes in handy to know someone almost all your life. Do you keep in touch with a friend like that?"

"I wish. All my close friends from childhood no longer live in Seven Oaks."

"Wasn't Henry a friend of yours? I seem to remember Edwina saying something about that," Maggie interjected into the conversation between Kane and Dr. Johnson.

Although surprised by her question, the president managed to say smoothly as if he'd practiced the answer, "Yes, a dear friend I will miss greatly. If you two will excuse me, I see a couple I need to greet." He rose and turned toward Kane. "Mingle. Remember those contributors."

After Dr. Johnson left, Kane drew closer to Maggie. "He certainly moved fast in his getaway."

"Are we going to have that effect on others tonight?"

"Only if they have something to hide."

"Let's mingle and see."

Kane scooted back his chair and stood, holding his hand out to Maggie. "Yes, ma'am. I'm at your service."

"Ah, I think I see Dr. Maples over there. I would know him anywhere from the photos I've seen of him. I didn't get to meet him last night at the barbecue, but I want to this evening."

"And I see he's with his wife. I heard a rumor floating around campus lately that he was engaged in a compromising relationship with a student. Should we rattle his cage?"

"By all means." Maggie watched the science professor speaking to his wife as they approached them. The woman bent close to her husband and her look, as she whispered something, was full of venom. "I would love to know what she just told Dr. Maples."

A few more steps and Maggie and Kane stopped in front of the pair.

Kane put a smile on his face. "I haven't had a chance to congratulate you on becoming the head for the science department. It's long overdue."

Mrs. Maples moved back from her husband, arranging her features into a neutral expression while Dr. Maples said, "Thanks. I've worked hard for the privilege."

His wife snorted. "Sam, I need a drink. Nice to see you, Kane." Then she hurried away before her husband could reply.

A flush colored the science professor's cheeks. "All that's happened lately with Henry's murder has really upset her."

"Yes, it's affected the whole town." Kane brought Maggie forward. "This is my date, Maggie Ridgeway. She's a speech therapist at the hospital."

After the professor shook her hand, Maggie said, "I've heard your classes are very popular. The students I've talked to who work at the hospital love your courses, especially several of the nurses who had you."

His blush deepened. "I love to teach. That's the only downside to being the department head. Some of the time I've spent teaching will be cut in the future."

"I'm sure the students will miss you. I told one of the nurses my interest in science, and she encouraged me to take one of your classes. She said something about how you take time out of your—er—busy schedule to help students who are having trouble with certain concepts, meeting with them after hours."

One of the professor's eyebrows quirked. "Isn't that what a teacher should do—impart their knowledge in a way a student will learn? Sometimes it takes a one-on-one session."

"We need more professors at the university level who'll spend time making sure their students understand," Maggie said in such an innocent voice she thought she should take up acting as a hobby.

Dr. Maples peered over toward the bar set up in the corner. "I'd better check on my wife. It was nice meeting you, Miss Ridgeway. Kane, see you around."

Maggie observed Dr. Maples as he scurried like the rat he was toward his wife. She could remember quizzing that nurse who had suggested taking a class about Dr. Maples. The young woman, who had just graduated from college last year, clammed up quickly when Maggie had probed her about those one-on-one sessions.

"Who should we scare off next?" Kane murmured close to her ear.

His presence so close sent a bolt of awareness down her. Suddenly sleuthing wasn't what she wanted to do. She wanted to be alone with him.

"Any suggestions?" she asked, her question coming out a little breathless.

"How about joining Thomas and Lisa Sellman? They're talking with Bradley and Beth."

"Do you really suspect Thomas? We haven't found any evidence in the apartment other than on Dr. Johnson and Dr. Maples."

"That doesn't mean there isn't more out there. Henry might not have left it around his apartment. He had a knack for making people angry at him."

"You did say that Henry messed up Thomas's chance for a scholarship that would have paid his last year of graduate school."

"And don't forget Beth dated Henry for a while, and it didn't end well."

"But that was several years ago. Why would she kill him now? I don't see her overpowering a man so much bigger than her."

"True." He planted his hand at the small of her back as he started forward. "But we really don't know what we're up against. We don't know if Henry was blackmailing anyone or not."

"I like Beth. And Lisa is my hair stylist. I don't want the murder to be connected to them."

"Neither do I. So let's prove it can't be Thomas or Beth."

"That I like." Maggie made a slight detour to grab her water from the table. Although the room was air-conditioned, she was hot. Grilling others was hard work.

"It's nice to see you all here tonight," Maggie said to the two couples when she joined them.

Lisa Sellman greeted Maggie with a smile. "I do Dr.

Johnson's wife's hair. She gave me free tickets to this event, so I couldn't pass up an evening with my husband. This is the first time I've been in the ballroom at the Seven Oaks Hotel. It's everything I've been told by my clients."

"Who's watching the twins?" Maggie settled in between Bradley and Kane.

"Edwina. She's such a dear. She insisted on it when she heard I got the tickets."

"That sounds like her. She's also watching Kenny and Ashley." Maggie took a sip of her water, welcoming the coolness sliding down her throat.

"I know Edwina from church. She's wonderful with the kids. She substitutes for any Sunday school teacher who is absent. Tyler talks about her all the time and enjoys it when she teaches his class," Beth said, looking stunning in a modest black gown that flared at her waist.

"You don't have long until graduation," Kane said to Thomas. "Have you decided what you're going to do next?"

The young man beamed. "Dr. Maples is helping me get a grant to work on my doctorate at Seven Oaks. I'll be working under his tutelage."

"That would never have happened with Dr. Payne," Lisa said, frowning. "I know I should feel sorry he was killed, but he didn't do my family any favors. Our life is much easier with the man gone."

Thomas shot his wife a look that shouted for her to be quiet.

Lisa ignored him and continued, "Whoever murdered Dr. Payne did the world a favor."

"Lisa," Thomas finally said, exasperated. "Don't you have to call and check on the twins? Didn't you tell Edwina you would and let her know when we'd be home?"

She sent him an annoyed glare. "I'm only saying what everyone is thinking. I have nothing to hide. Kane, you have to agree our apartment building is much nicer with the man gone. This past year or so the tension was so thick you could slice it with a knife." Lisa sipped her light-brown-colored drink. "In fact, ever since he moved in, people went out of their way to avoid him. The only one who would even speak to him was Edwina, and she never gives up on anyone. I wish I could be like her, but I can't."

Maggie didn't know about how it was before she'd moved in, but the anxiety level for her was high since she'd come to live at Twin Oaks Apartments.

Thomas grasped his wife's hand, taking her glass and setting it on a tray of a waiter passing by. "Excuse us."

After the young man escorted his wife toward the lobby, Bradley blew out a breath. "She certainly unloaded."

"Can you blame her?" Beth asked, watching Lisa and Thomas disappear in the crowd.

"I know the professors in the science department are breathing easier." Bradley shifted closer to Beth, slipping her hand within his. "I interact with all the departments, and I can tell you the impact of Henry's arrival at Seven Oaks University was strongly felt."

Beth frowned. "If you all don't mind, let's not talk about Henry Payne."

"I can certainly understand after what he did to you." Maggie hated baiting Beth, but she needed to know if the woman was capable of murder.

"You mean his public humiliation of me. I wouldn't want that to happen to me again, but I have moved on. If the Lord forgives us our sins, I can forgive Henry for what he did in the middle of the student union."

Maggie shot Kane a glance. She hadn't heard of this, but she wouldn't ask Beth about it. She would talk to Kane, though, later.

"Vicky and John just arrived. I was getting worried about them. They were supposed to be right behind us." Kane waved to the couple to join them.

As Vicky and her husband weaved their way toward them, pausing a few times to speak to some guests, Maggie assessed Beth. She was right about forgiveness, but Maggie wasn't sure she could forgive her birth mother. She was trying, but unless she came out and asked her why she'd given her up, she didn't think it was truly possible.

"What happened to you two?" Kane asked, pulling Maggie's thoughts to the present.

"The snake got loose in the apartment, so we went on a hunt to find it because I refuse to come home and find it somewhere unexpected later," Vicky said.

The conversation quickly revolved around children and what they could do to change plans at the last moment. Even Kane had a few stories to tell about babysitting Ashley and Kenny. The sense of being on the outside looking in swamped Maggie as it so often had while growing up.

Fifteen minutes later, Dr. Johnson announced that dinner was being served. Throughout the meal, Kane did his best to court the contributors at the table. Maggie thought as she watched Dr. Johnson and Kane conversing it was as if she were observing a wrestling match where the participants tag teamed.

That image stayed in her mind through the rest of the evening until she encountered David in the lobby as Kane went to retrieve her shawl from the coatroom.

"Tell me you're close to solving the murder," she said to the detective.

"No. I've checked into the information you two have given me concerning Dr. Johnson and Dr. Maples, but there isn't enough there to point to either one."

"What about the connection of the two arson fires—the Johnsons' house and my apartment."

"They didn't start the same way. I'm not sure there's a connection." The look David gave Maggie was full of regret. "I'm sorry. There was little physical evidence and no witnesses who have come forward. I'm wading through the long list of people who weren't happy with Henry. That's all I've got to go on."

"I know you're doing your best. Not all murders are solved within an hour like on television."

"How about none." David peered at Kane strolling toward them with her black shawl hanging over his arm. "Are you two leaving now?"

"Yes," Maggie answered while Kane draped the wrap over her shoulders.

"I've had enough of large crowds to last me half a year." Kane looked about him. "Where's your date?"

"What date? I came alone tonight."

"I thought you were going out with that elementary school teacher."

"She's just a friend. Good night you two. I probably won't be long myself."

As Maggie walked beside Kane toward his car in the parking lot at the side of the hotel, a feeling of being watched froze her. She peered back and saw a dark shadow at one of the windows on the second floor near the ballroom entrance. She came to a stop and pivoted. The figure ducked back.

"What's wrong?" Kane asked, winding his arm around her as coldness burrowed into her bones.

"I think someone was watching us."

"Does that surprise you? I think we ruffled a few feathers tonight."

"Speaking of ruffling feathers, what did Henry do to Beth in the student union?"

"I won't repeat the unkind words he called Beth in front of staff and students, but she barely made it out of the building before she broke down."

How awful. Maggie's heart went out to the woman. Amazing. She'd managed somehow to forgive Henry. Or, had Beth really?

When she had a break between seeing patients on Monday morning, Maggie punched in the number left by Mr. Alexander of a Nashville law firm. His secretary put her right through.

"Ms. Ridgeway, I'm so glad you got in touch with me. I represent Dr. Henry Payne."

She stiffened. "Why do you want to talk to me?"

"I've been out of the country on an extended vacation and only recently I learned that Henry passed away."

"Someone killed him."

"Yes, I know he was murdered. Anyway, the reason I need to see you is that you're in his will."

Henry Payne's? "I don't understand. I don't know the man. How could I be in his will? You've got the wrong person."

"I don't know the answer to why Henry has you in his will, but I haven't made a mistake. You're the right person."

"I don't want anything from *that* man."

"Most of the money he has is being left to the Southside Recreational Center, but there's one thing he wanted you to have."

"What?" The picture of the man she'd come to know over the past few weeks warred with the image of someone who left his money to a charity.

"It's a key to a safety deposit box. The contents of the box were willed to you. I was to hand you the key in person. The bank is here in Nashville."

Maggie sank into a chair nearby, her hand holding the phone trembling. It was too much to take in. Why her? How did Henry know her? What was in the box?

"Can we arrange a time for you to get your inheritance?"

No! I don't want anything from that monster! "I…"

What's in the safety deposit box? What if there are more flash drives? Can I turn my back on that?

"I can be there tomorrow afternoon say around two," she finally said, her whole body shaking now.

"That's fine."

After Mr. Alexander gave her directions to his office, Maggie snapped her cell closed and dropped it into her lap. She stared at the beige wall in front of her as though it held answers to the questions flying around in her mind.

But the one that overrode all the others embedded itself into her thoughts until she wanted to scream. *How did Henry know me?*

"You don't know how relieved I am that you came with me," Maggie said as she got off the elevator on the fifth floor of the office building in Nashville.

"You still can't figure out why Henry would leave you a key to a safety deposit box?" Kane held open the door for her to the Alexander and Cussler Law Firm.

"No."

The receptionist immediately showed Maggie and Kane to Mr. Alexander's office. The lawyer came around his desk and shook hands with both of them, then gestured for them to take a seat.

When Mr. Alexander sat again, he pulled a drawer open and withdrew an envelope. "This is to a box at the First Tennessee Bank. You're on the account as well as Henry and I."

"I am? Do you know what's in it?"

"No, but I was to see that the contents got to the proper person—you. I was added by Henry in case I couldn't find you."

"But I live in his apartment."

The man frowned. "You do? I didn't realize that. I did know you'd moved to Seven Oaks recently."

"How?" Puzzled, Maggie glanced at Kane for any insight, but all that greeted her was his neutral expression.

"I called your mother to find out where you were since the last number Henry gave me didn't work. He also gave me your mother's. She told me you moved to Seven Oaks and how to get in touch with you."

But her adoptive mother hadn't bothered to let her know that a lawyer was looking for her. The woman hadn't bothered to call her once since she'd moved to Seven Oaks. A knife twisted into her heart. All she'd ever wanted was her mother's love. "Why did Henry leave me anything? I didn't even know him."

Mr. Alexander rose and handed the envelope to her. "I suggest you go to the bank and find out. I'm not privy to what's in it, and I don't want to postulate what it is."

"Mr. Alexander, does Henry Payne have any relatives that would want his personal possessions? I have them stored down in my basement." Kane pushed to his feet at the same time Maggie did.

"The will states that except for everything in the safety deposit box, the rest of his estate goes to Southside Recreational Center. I suppose the items belong to them."

"Thank you, Mr. Alexander." Maggie stuffed the envelope into her purse.

Out in the hallway she dropped her head, her hands clutched around the top of her bag. "This doesn't make any sense."

"Are you sure you didn't know Henry? Maybe you helped him at the hospital or some other time."

"No. I've seen his picture many times. I don't forget faces. I've never seen him."

Kane strode the few paces to the elevator and punched the down button. "Then all we can do is go to the bank and find out what's in that box. I noticed the address on the front of the envelope. We'll get directions downstairs with the building receptionist."

Five minutes later, Maggie climbed into Kane's car. A cold sweat blanketed her face. She swiped her hand across her forehead, but instantly more perspiration popped out on her skin. She didn't like this one bit. Something was wrong with this whole situation.

What if Henry discovered Vicky's secret and had been blackmailing her birth mother? What if he had been the person who had anonymously tipped her off about Vicky Pennington? If that were the case, how could her secret remain a secret? What if Vicky had something to do with Henry's murder?

Her head throbbed with her unanswered questions. When Kane parked next to the bank, she hugged the handle as though that could stop the door opening and what was to come.

"Let's leave," she said, a frantic tone to her words.

"You can't. What if the information can lead to the murderer? You aren't safe until he's found."

He was right. She had to do this, and if the secret came out, then she would deal with the repercussions with the Lord by her side.

Maybe this is Your will. Keeping her identity from Vicky and her siblings had been so hard on her. Maybe she was wrong not to say anything. Confusion reigned as she exited Kane's car.

"Let's get this over with." She trudged toward the building as though she were walking to her doom.

As the woman at the bank showed her where the safety deposit box was and fit both keys into their proper slot, Maggie's stomach roiled. When she carried the container to the table, her palms dampened until she thought the metal box would slip from her grasp.

"Do you want me to leave?"

Kane's question dangled before Maggie, giving her an out if the worst was revealed—that she was Vicky's daughter. Tired of running from the truth, she shook her head. Her hands trembled as she lifted the lid.

She stared at the stacks of hundred dollar bills in most of the large box with a leather pouch at the front. Picking up one bundle of cash, she flipped through it. "I've never seen so much money." Then she thought of how Henry might have gotten the currency—through blackmail—and dropped the wad of bills back into the container.

"I would estimate close to a quarter of a million dollars."

Blood money probably. She wanted nothing to do with it. Gingerly she grasped the worn leather pouch and opened it. The first piece of paper was a birth certificate. The state seal marked the back with raised lines.

Slowly, her hands shaking so badly she lost her grip on the paper once, she spread the sheet on the table to reveal her worst fear. In bold black letters her name was splashed across the top.

"Who's Mary Stanton? Why would Henry have her birth certificate?"

"It's Mary Margaret Stanton, and that's me." Her voice roughened with each word until the last of the sentence was spoken in a raw whisper.

"You! Why would Henry…" Kane's gaze latched onto what Maggie saw on the certificate. Both her parents' names.

"Victoria Stanton is your mother and Henry Payne is your father. Vicky Pennington? I seem to recall her talking about her father and using the name Stanton."

"I'm afraid so." Her gaze remained glued to Henry's name as though it were a neon sign on Main Street announcing she was the daughter of a man everyone hated.

"I—I don't know what to say." Kane plopped into a chair near the table.

With a violent shake of her head—as if that could rid her of the truth—she stuffed the money then the pouch into her oversized purse. "Let's get out of here." She sucked in a deep breath, but her lungs constricted from lack of oxygen-rich air.

Leaving the safety deposit box on the table along with the key, she whirled around and started for the door. The room spun before her. She clutched the wall nearby and nearly went to her knees.

Closing her eyes, she tried to calm her rapid heartbeat. But the thundering in her head continued. Although Kane stood next to her, saying something, she couldn't make out his words.

Suddenly her bag weighed her down, and she sank to the tile floor. She hugged the purse to her chest and forced air into her lungs. Over and over. Slowly the room quit rotating.

She looked up at Kane hovering nearby. His stone-cold expression stole her thoughts.

"Maggie, you've been lying this whole time."

ELEVEN

Maggie rose, gripping her purse. Her eyes narrowed on Kane's face. "I never lied to you. I knew nothing about Henry Payne. Yes, I knew Vicky was my birth mother, but it isn't my place to spread that news around. We never once talked about the woman who gave birth to me and gave me up. So how do you think I lied to you?"

"How about to Vicky then? Doesn't she deserve to know who you are?"

"No. She gave that right up twenty-eight years ago."

Kane stiffened, the action bringing forth Maggie's guilt of late that she should never have come to Seven Oaks.

"What about her husband? He doesn't know about me. I'm almost one hundred percent sure she never told him. Then let's not forget Ashley and Kenny. I come marching into their lives and change everything. I won't be responsible for that." Who was she trying to convince—Kane or herself?

He thrust his face into hers. "Then why did you come to Seven Oaks in the first place, if not to cause trouble?"

His words hurt—deeply. More than she wished. After all they had shared, did he really think she had only come to cause trouble for Vicky?

"What business is this of yours?"

"John and Vicky are close friends. I owe John my life, and I won't see it destroyed by anyone."

A thought came unbidden into her mind. "Does that include Henry? Where were you the evening he was murdered?" The need to strike out at Kane overrode all common sense.

Everything about him conveyed anger—his stance, his look and even his breathing, which was short, shallow inhalations. "Let's go. It's a several-hour drive back to Seven Oaks."

He pivoted and exited the safety deposit room. He didn't glance back once as she trailed him to his car. He sat behind the steering wheel drumming his fingers against it. The second she closed the vehicle's door, he started his engine and screeched out of the parking lot.

For the next three hours Kane didn't say a word. He didn't look at her either. His jawline hardened into a forbidden expression that vied with the coldness that encased her.

When he pulled up to the apartment building and parked, he finally asked, "What are you going to do?"

She grasped the handle, her fingernails digging into her palm. "I don't know. Whether you want to believe it or not, this is something I hadn't expected. I don't want Henry as my father. He isn't. I had a wonderful adoptive father who loved me."

"What about Vicky?"

She shifted her gaze to his face. Through a sheen of tears, she glimpsed the same icy demeanor as when they headed back to Seven Oaks. The temperature in the car plunged as did her hopes that Kane would understand her pain and confusion.

"As I told you before, none of this is up to me. It's Vicky's story. I would never do anything to hurt the children."

"You already have by coming here and living a lie. You're their sister—part of their family—whether anyone wants it or not."

Maggie shoved the door open. "I can't talk about this now."

She rushed to the porch, fumbled for her house key and quickly let herself inside as the sound of Kane's car door shutting slammed through her.

She couldn't go to Edwina's, not as distraught as she was, so she hurried up the staircase to the second floor and entered her partially redone apartment. The scent of smoke still lingered, but it wasn't as strong. The restoration company had another week until they said they would be finished. How was she going to pretend everything was all right? All her plans were ruined. Her life was a shambles.

She strode into her kitchen, tossed the pouch on the table as though it had burned her palms and opened a window along the back of the house. She started to turn away when she glimpsed Kane walking toward the lake. She'd needed his support, his understanding, and he hadn't been able to give it to her. All he saw was a woman out to destroy the life John had forged for his family in Seven Oaks. And as she watched him at the edge of the water, his hands stuffed into his pockets, his shoulders slumped forward, she couldn't blame Kane for those thoughts. If John discovered Vicky's secret, she didn't know if the proud man would stay with his wife.

Vicky is Maggie's mother. Henry is her father.

Kane's head ached from trying to grapple with that news. What would this do to his friend's family? He'd promised himself he would be there for John whenever he needed him, just as John had been there for him in Iraq.

A light breeze from the south blew off the water, causing some ripples in its surface. What kind of ripples would the news that Vicky had a baby with Henry and Maggie was her daughter cause?

He hunched his shoulders, the coolness in the wind heightening the cold sensation he'd experienced since Maggie had revealed her secret.

"Maggie." Her name escaped his lips on a sigh.

He'd started to—care about her, beyond friendship. How could he trust her now?

Her secret could destroy the man who saved his life, could tear apart his family.

Lord, is this why I lived when so many didn't, so I could be here to help John through this? Is this my purpose?

He still didn't know why he'd survived when others hadn't. In his dreams—no, nightmares—he heard their screams as they'd died among the rubble of the bombed building.

But John had found him and carried him to safety before the ceiling had collapsed. It would have finished him off, and he'd seen it from a distance—had known the other still-trapped soldiers had died.

Shuddering, he dropped his head, staring at the shore where the water lapped against his shoes. He'd begun to trust again. He'd actually thought he could have a future with a woman. But not now. Not ever. Maggie had killed that as surely as the day Ruth had walked away.

"Edwina said I would probably find you up here."

Maggie spun around at the sound of Kane's voice. The same cold mask as she'd seen earlier on the ride back from Nashville carved his features in hardness. She had nothing else to say to him. Saying she was sorry wasn't what he wanted to hear and at this point would do nothing to melt his anger.

His mouth tightened. "There were other papers in the leather pouch. Have you looked at them yet?"

She shook her head. She hadn't thought about anything except the birth certificate and what it meant to her.

"Then we should look at them in case there's any evidence

that might point to who killed Henry." His gaze narrowed slightly on her. "Of course, you can do it alone if you think there's anything else you want to hide that might be revealed."

Her heart bled at his harsh words. "There isn't anything." She gestured to where the pouch lay. "You can take a look."

He stepped to the kitchen table and flinched as he touched the birth certificate. Quickly he moved it to the side and perused the next paper.

Hold me. Tell me I'm not anything like Henry.

Maggie pressed her folded arms to her, but nothing she did warmed her. "What does it say?"

He didn't answer right away, and Maggie started to move toward him when Kane lifted his gaze to hers.

"This is Henry's account of what really happened the night that Dr. Johnson and his wife died in the house fire. And he says that if anything happens to him that is suspicious for you to take this to the police. He accuses Phillip Johnson of killing his father and mother."

"What?" Maggie covered the distance between them and took the paper. "Phillip's father was a mean drunk who abused his son when he was drinking. Phillip had told Henry how much he hated his parents. He took care of the problem by burning down the house. Henry states that his friend didn't show up at his house until thirty minutes after the fire, although Henry had told the police he'd been there all night," she said, stunned that a thirteen-year-old could kill his parents.

"There's more." Kane read another sheet Henry penned. "There are records of injuries to Phillip as a child. An old audiotape of Phillip talking about his father and how much he hated him. Also Henry says on the tape there's a place where Phillip dreams of getting rid of his father and how he would do it—dousing him in alcohol and lighting him up. Henry hadn't thought Phillip was the arsonist because he was supposedly spying on his love interest at a girlfriend's sleepover and his dad hadn't died like Phillip had envisioned. So when his friend begged him to tell the police he was there the whole evening, Henry did."

Maggie looked down at the pouch and saw several photos of two young boys, some the same ones as she saw on the flash drive. Flipping through them, she sucked in a deep breath. "These are pictures of a boy acting as though he was setting another on fire up to the point of actually doing it. I think it's Henry who played the dad, so I'm guessing the other child is Phillip."

"Sick."

That word reverberated through Maggie. That was her biological father. "Why are there photos and a tape?"

"Obviously Henry started young taking pictures of others doing unsavory things."

The sarcasm in Kane's voice reinforced how hopeless the whole situation was. She'd come to have deep feelings for him, and now she was destroying that.

Am I going to continuously pay for my mother's mistake, Lord?

Tears smarted her eyes while Kane snapped open his cell and placed a call to David.

"We've got some evidence about not only Henry's murder but the Johnsons' arson case. Can you come over to Maggie's?" Kane paused. "Yeah. The information is explosive. See you in a bit."

Maggie strode into the living room, needing to put some distance between her and the pouch. If Dr. Johnson killed his parents and Henry, this would rip the town apart.

"David will be here in a few minutes. You need to go through the pouch and take out what doesn't pertain to the murders." Kane approached her, holding it out for her.

"Yes, we don't need to have it plastered all over the newspaper about Vicky and Henry."

"What are you going to do with that information? David will want to know why you have this and how you got it. I won't lie to my friend, even to protect another."

What she had been struggling with for the last couple of weeks was decided for her. "We'll tell David I'm Henry's daughter and about the lawyer contacting me."

"When the news gets around, Vicky will know who you are."

"Yes. It'll be in her hands then. I won't say anything about being Vicky's daughter to David or anyone else. It isn't important to the case."

"Are you prepared for the press and people's reactions?"

"Why do you care? It's my problem, not yours. I'll be safe and soon out of your hair."

"You're leaving Twin Oaks?"

"I'm leaving Seven Oaks. I'll give my two weeks' notice tomorrow at work. I can't stay with everyone knowing I'm Henry's daughter. He was a monster. I've seen your reaction to the news."

He fisted his hands, his jaw clenching. "My reaction isn't to that fact but to the other."

"I can't change either fact now. Hopefully if John doesn't know about me, their marriage will be okay."

"So you're going to walk away from Kenny and Ashley? I've seen how you are with them."

She loved her siblings, and that part hurt the most. "I'm sure Vicky will want that. She never wanted me in the first place so why now." Maggie took the evidence that David needed out of the pouch and gave it to Kane.

"Vicky was a teenager. Maybe she didn't really have a choice. Have you ever considered her in all this?"

Maggie winced. "You're defending her?"

"Aren't you the one who told me to forgive Ruth? That forgiveness would start me on the road to recovery. Well, if that's good for me, then it should be for you."

"Have you really forgiven Ruth?" Maggie put the leather pouch behind a photo of her adoptive father on the mantel behind her.

"It's a work in progress."

"I'm so glad you're learning to forgive." *Because I could use it.* But when she peered into Kane's expression, she saw no forgiveness for her.

A movement by the front door drew Maggie's attention. She strode forward. "Thanks for coming, David. You might want to take a seat while I explain how I came by this evidence."

Friday afternoon Maggie dragged herself into the apartment building, mentally and physically exhausted with the past few days' events. The news broke last night about her being Henry's daughter and the recent developments in the Payne murder investigation. Today she'd learned that Dr. Phillip Johnson had been arrested for his parents' murders as well as being the prime suspect in Henry's murder.

Everyone in Seven Oaks was talking about the news. As predicted, it rocked the college town. Only a handful at the hospital had approached her about the evidence she'd supplied to the police, and then they hadn't mentioned why she had it. But she heard the whispers as she'd walked down the corridors of the hospital.

Maggie plodded to Edwina's apartment, her head pulsating against her skull almost as badly as it had with the concussion. Before she had a chance to knock, the older woman swung her door open.

"I saw you from the window."

The look on Edwina's face didn't bode well for her. Her

mouth pulled tightly together and tension came off her in waves. "What's wrong?"

"Vicky's in the kitchen, and she's distraught. I can usually calm her down, but I can't this time. She's not leaving until she talks to you. I'm worried about her. She looks awful."

"I know what this is about. Is it possible for me to talk to her alone?"

"Sure. Since John isn't home, I'll go up to her apartment and keep an eye on the kids."

Edwina started to leave. Maggie placed her hand on her friend's arm and said, "Thanks for not asking the obvious question."

"You'll tell me when and if you need a friendly ear. You certainly don't need any more grief, child."

Maggie closed the door and fell back against it, trying to gather her thoughts concerning finally having the talk she should have had from the very beginning. After visiting the church and counseling with her pastor, she realized that. Secrets didn't remain hidden forever. How had she thought she could merrily come into Vicky's life, then go on about her way when she got the information she wanted?

Lord, I was so wrong. Please help me to right this situation. My anger drove me to do something I shouldn't have. I'm so sorry. Please forgive me.

With a deep sigh, Maggie made her way into the kitchen. When she entered, Vicky looked up, her eyes red with deep circles under them. Her haggard face firmed into a frown.

"Why didn't you tell me who you were?" Vicky's hands clamped about a mug that she carefully set on the table.

Maggie eased into the chair across from her birth mother. "Because I didn't want you to know." She shifted her gaze to the window, bright light streaming through to the pattern across the tile. "You'd rejected me once. I didn't want to give you a second chance."

"Then why did you come to Seven Oaks? Why did you move in across the hall?" Fury laced each of Vicky's questions and struck Maggie as if she'd been slapped.

"You mean into my father's apartment." Her own anger rose. She was sorry about how the situation had been handled, but she couldn't seem to get past her anger to forgive—not when she thought of who her father was, of the pain of her childhood, the rejection she faced over and over growing up.

"I've had a lot of regrets and that definitely is one. Henry was a charmer."

"Besides being a monster and my dad?"

"He wasn't always like that. At fifteen his aunt, who he lived with, died, and he was left an orphan again. But that time there were no other relatives to take him in. He went into foster care. He began to change."

"It seems I have something in common with my father."

"You were adopted. I made my parents promise that would happen."

"Which time are you talking about? My first adoptive parents were abusive and neglectful, according to the records. I was removed from their home by the state. They couldn't put me up for adoption until all parental rights had been terminated, which meant I lived in foster homes for several years. Finally I could be adopted by the Ridgeways when I was seven. I ended up with a great father and a mother who didn't really want me. Isn't that ironic? Two mothers who didn't want me and that isn't even counting my first adoptive mother."

Vicky paled. "I didn't know. I was sixteen when I had you, and I was afraid. I'd been sent away from Seven Oaks by my parents to have the baby in Louisville. They didn't want anyone to know I had one. They were so ashamed." Her voice caught on the last word. "I didn't even tell Henry. It was at the beginning of the summer. I picked a fight with him and told him I wanted to date others. I hadn't started showing yet, so I was able to go away for the summer and come back to start the school year without anyone being the wiser."

"How did Henry find out?"

"I'm not sure. He was always so observant. He may have known I was pregnant and didn't say anything. He never told me how he figured it out, but when he came back to Seven Oaks, he let me know he knew what I'd done all those years ago." Vicky shivered, cupping the mug but not picking it up. "He was furious at me. I thought he would tell John, but he didn't. I kept waiting for him to."

"So John doesn't know about me?"

"No, I could never tell him. I had done something wrong, and he thought I was perfect when we met. As the years passed, it became harder to say anything. He's a man of integrity and…"

"In other words, you were ashamed of me because your parents made you feel that way."

"No. No." Vicky waved her hand in the air. "I wasn't ashamed of you. I was ashamed of myself for giving in to Henry. I reaped the repercussions."

"No, I did." Maggie rose. She couldn't do this any longer. "I won't say anything to John. It's your place to do that, but a word of advice from your other daughter. Recently I've learned painfully that secrets will eat at you until they erode your moral fiber. Now if you don't mind, I'm exhausted."

Vicky tried to approach her, but Maggie backed away.

"Even from the grave, Henry has affected my life. I thought with his death that threat was gone."

How many others felt that way? Obviously, Dr. Johnson had. As Vicky turned to leave, Maggie said, "While I'm still here, I would love to see Ashley and Kenny. I won't say anything to them about who I am. Will you allow me to?"

"Yes, they would wonder why you didn't see them all of a sudden."

After her birth mother disappeared into the other room, Maggie sank back against the counter, gripping its edge. *I thought with his death that threat was gone.*

Those words bombarded her. Did the police have the wrong person for Henry's murder? What if it had been Vicky, trying to quiet her tormentor finally?

Was she safe as she had thought with Phillip Johnson's arrest?

TWELVE

As Maggie jogged back from the park, her sneakers striking the pavement in a rhythmic sound momentarily lulled her into a sense all was right with the world. Until flashes from the past few days intruded into her mind. Then she remembered the mess she'd made of her life. The tension—silent and menacing—in the building had eaten through any defenses she'd managed to erect.

She was falling in love with Kane, and he wanted nothing to do with her. That had become apparent yesterday when he'd looked straight through her in the foyer of the apartment building. Was she her father's daughter—tinkering with people's lives in order to control the situation?

Why, Lord? Why was Henry my biological father? I feel dirty. It's bad enough I was conceived out of wedlock, but to have a monster as a father…

The very thought shook her to her core. She pushed herself harder, faster.

At least over this weekend she could avoid people. She hadn't even gone to church with Edwina this morning. She couldn't deal with the whispers and stares. But tomorrow she would have to go into work and face everyone. Although she sweated from her exertion, a shiver shimmied down her length, raising goose bumps.

She turned the corner to the street where Twin Oaks sat at the end. Its massive structure drew her like Lorelei enticed sailors to run their ships aground. Suddenly she came to a decision as she neared the building.

Slowing her pace, she took the steps to the porch two at a time and unlocked the door. When she entered, quiet ruled. She paused and drank in the silence, trying to draw solace from it.

At the sound of a door slamming upstairs, she jerked around toward the staircase. Heavy footsteps, as if the angry person was walking quickly, preceded John's appearance at the top of the stairs. His gaze locked with hers and narrowed on her.

He knew. She could read it in his face, a face forged with pain. For a few seconds she thought about whirling around and escaping back outside.

He stomped down the steps and honed in on her. His mouth tightened in a grim line, his eyes blazing. When he stopped in front of her, almost invading her personal space, she straightened. She deserved everything he gave her.

"Why did you come here?" But instead of rage, agony coated each word. "Do you know what you've done?"

She flinched back. No response that would make him feel better came to mind.

John opened his mouth to say something but snapped it shut without speaking. He pivoted and hurried toward the front door. It rattled as he shut it.

Lord, I tried to avoid this. I didn't want this. Really. Kenny and Ashley deserved a loving family environment. Please help me fix this somehow.

She stared at the front door for a long moment, trying to figure out what to do next. Should she go see Vicky? She would be devastated by John's response to her news. Should she go after John and try to explain? Explain what? That his wife had a child out of wedlock and had never told him. That he really didn't know his wife as well as he thought. That she had been living a lie for years.

Or should she just pack her bags and escape?

No, she couldn't, wouldn't do that yet. She knew what she should do.

She quickly headed for the basement before she changed her mind. Kane might be able to help John; then she would go see Vicky.

Dread leadened her steps as she neared his apartment. Kane answered on the fourth knock as if he had debated with himself whether to open the door to her.

His eyebrow rose, but he didn't say a word. Folding his arms over his chest, he fixed her with a cold stare.

She hooked her hair behind her ears; then she rubbed her damp palms together. Anxiety swelled in her throat until she didn't know if she could speak.

She swallowed hard several times. "I need to talk to you about John. Vicky told him who I am, and he didn't take it well."

The coldness melted some to be replaced with concern. "Do you blame him? He told me once he'd told Vicky everything about himself—even the fact he tried drugs in high school. He'd always thought she had shared herself totally. He thought that was what was important in a good marriage. Now your appearance has undermined that for him. The very foundation of his marriage is built on sand, not rock."

"That was never my intention."

"C'mon. Are you so sure of that? You must hate Vicky. Why not break up her marriage as payback."

The contempt in his voice eroded her composure. "I won't tell you that didn't cross my mind, but I never really considered that option, partially because I wouldn't do that to Kenny and Ashley, but mostly because that isn't the type of person I am." *Can't you see I'm not my father's daughter?*

He dropped his arms to his sides. "Why are you here?"

"John stormed out of here. I think he needs someone to talk to. I thought you might be that someone—that is if you know where he went."

Concern filled his expression totally now. "I think I do." He stepped out into the hall, closed his door and made his way to the stairs. "What about Vicky?"

"I'm going to talk with her. See if she's all right."

Kane threw her an unreadable look. "You are? This has got to be sweet revenge."

"Revenge was never my motive."

"What was?"

"When my adoptive father died, that last time I talked with him, he suggested I try and locate my birth mother. He knew how his wife felt about me. She hadn't wanted a child. He had, but because he wouldn't be around, he wanted me to have a family. He'd hoped it would be my biological one. I'd promised him I would try because for years I'd wondered about the woman who had given birth to me."

At the top of the stairs Kane faced her. "Well, you've fulfilled the promise and managed to damage a good marriage in the process."

The icy facade had returned to his features. "Hopefully when I leave here, they'll be able to mend their marriage. If it's as good as you say, they should be able to."

"So you are leaving?"

Something flickered behind the cold mask, but it was so fleeting she wasn't sure of what she saw. "Yes. In fact, I've gone ahead and gotten a room in the dorm for the next week. I should have most of my things out of here by tomorrow evening." She pushed past him to go up to Vicky's.

His words stopped her halfway across the foyer. "David called. In Dr. Johnson's wife's car trunk the police found a man's blue shirt with a torn pocket that matched the fabric Henry had been clutching in his hand. She was supposed to have taken some clothes to Goodwill and had stuck them in a bag then forgot about them. Dr. Johnson denies owning that shirt, and his wife doesn't remember…but she did say she didn't know what her husband was doing that night. She had been sleeping soundly for the first time in a while."

With her back to Kane she said, "Good. This whole episode is finally coming to an end with the killer caught." She started up the stairs to the second floor. She would have her life back soon. Without threats to her safety. Without Seven Oaks. Without Kane.

When Maggie knocked on her birth mother's apartment, Ashley opened the door, tears streaming down her face. The child threw herself into Maggie's arms.

"Mommy's crying in her bedroom. I don't know what to do."

"Where's Kenny?" Maggie held her sister tightly, relishing the chance.

"He's still at Sean's I guess. I got bored and came home early."

"Where are you supposed to be?"

"Downstairs at the Sellmans'."

Maggie looked down at the child, combing her hair behind her ears. "Do me a favor. I'll talk to your mom while you go back to the Sellmans'. Okay?"

"But Mommy isn't happy."

"I know. But maybe I can make things better, and then she'll come get you."

A pout tugging at her mouth, Ashley nodded.

After the little girl left, Maggie made her way to Vicky's bedroom door and knocked. "Vicky, please let's talk."

Half a minute later she faced her mother. "Ashley let me in. She's concerned about you."

Vicky dabbed her eyes with a tissue, but they immediately filled with tears. "She should be downstairs."

"She is now, but I promised her I would talk to you. She's worried about you."

"I've made a mess of everything." Vicky turned back into her bedroom. "John will probably leave me. You hate me. I…"

Maggie moved inside and closed the door. "John loves you. I've seen it. Yes, he's mad and upset right now, but you two can work this out." She paused, trying to piece together her own feelings toward her biological mother.

Vicky sank onto her bed, her eyes huge with her sorrow. "But you'll never be able to forgive me for what I did to you years ago?"

Let it go. Anger and hate destroy. Forgiveness is the only option if you ever want to be free to live your own life. She'd been telling herself that for the past few days since her last meeting with Vicky when she hadn't been able to contain the emotions she'd carried around for so many years. She wanted to forgive Vicky then but hadn't been able to. Could she now?

"I thought at the time I was doing the right thing. My parents were ashamed of me and would never have accepted you. I was still in high school with no means of making a living on my own. I wanted to give you a better life. I didn't know it would turn out to be so bad for you."

Did it really? I had a wonderful father who loved me unconditionally. My adoptive mother had done her best and had never openly shown her true feelings until after my father passed away.

Lord, I need Your help. Please give me the strength to do what's right.

"It wasn't all bad. Henry may be my biological father, but he really isn't my father in my heart. The one who raised me, helped shape me into the person I am today, showed me the power of the Lord. He's my real father." Maggie drew in a fortifying breath, a peace she'd been seeking washing over her. "I can't hate you, Vicky. I forgive you for giving me up when I was born. You did the best you could under the circumstances."

"You forgive me?"

"Yes, and if I can forgive you, then so can John. Give him some time to accept the news."

"I was so wrong to keep that from him. I should have told him the truth from the beginning of our marriage, but I felt ashamed. I thought he wouldn't love me."

Maggie crossed the room and sat beside her mother. "You were sixteen and made a mistake. Everyone makes mistakes. Look at what I did. I should never have come here."

"Then I would never know about you." Vicky looked at her. "You've grown up to be a nice young lady. I used to dream about you and how well you'd turn out. I never forgot you. Ever." She put her hand over her heart. "I just carried you around in here secretly."

"But secrets have a way of poisoning things. I came here with a secret, and look what happened."

"Yeah, look what happened with my secret. When Henry had first returned to Seven Oaks to the very apartment building I lived in, I knew it was only a matter of time before John discovered I'd had a baby, but I couldn't bring myself to say anything. I kept thinking maybe Henry had changed into the young man I'd thought I loved at one time, but he hadn't. He was full of bitterness when he left Seven Oaks, and it had gotten worse over the years."

"Henry had his own secrets that came back to haunt him."

Vicky pushed off the bed. "I still can't believe that Dr. Johnson murdered him. That he'd killed his parents, too. So much is coming out now that my head aches."

"I know what you mean. Although the police haven't formally charged him with Henry's murder, only his parents'. David says it's only a matter of time before they do." Maggie rose, awed that she was in the same room with her mother with no secrets between them anymore. Maybe one day they would have a true mother/daughter relationship even if it had to be long distance. "I'd better go. I told Ashley you would come get her after I talked to you. I don't want her to worry any more than she already has."

Vicky walked with her as she headed for the hallway. "I will be telling my children you're their sister. I won't keep any more secrets. They deserve to know who you are, and you deserve to be in their life."

"I'm leaving, Vicky. I'm moving back to the dorm. I've given the hospital my two-week notice. I'm returning to St. Louis."

"No, you can't!" Stopping at the door, she placed a hand on Maggie. "What about Kenny, Ashley?"

"I can't stay. I…" How could she explain about her feelings concerning Kane? He didn't want her around reminding him of Ruth. She couldn't be around him seeing his contempt.

"Is this about Kane?"

Her throat tight, Maggie nodded.

"You've been so good for my children but also for Kane. I've never seen him become so involved with others like he is with you. He used to come home from his job and hide out in his workshop. He threw everything into the pieces of furniture he made. He hasn't really participated in life since he came back from the war."

Maggie wrenched the door open. "I just can't be where I'm not wanted. I'm sorry." She hurried toward the staircase. Her decision had been made. Talking about it only brought pain.

Kane saw John sitting on a bench that was secluded from prying eyes by a ring of tall bushes. His friend sat with his elbows on his thighs, his hands clasped as he stared at the small lake at the north end of the park. Kane's leg ached from practically jogging over to the place. He needed to get his other prosthesis out of its box in the closet the next time he decided to go for a run. It was time he got his old life back.

When Kane took a seat next to John, he slid his glance toward Kane then back to the water. "I see Vicky got you to come talk to me."

"Nope."

"She didn't?" He straightened and stared at Kane. "Then why are you here?"

"Maggie asked me to come talk to you."

"She did?" John snorted and resumed his study of the lake. "She's caused quite a commotion in my life."

Did Maggie really cause it? She wasn't responsible for what happened at her birth and after concerning Vicky. "For the longest time I've been so angry at Ruth for walking out on me when I needed her the most. That anger wouldn't allow me to see anything beyond that. Lately I've been taking a good hard look at that time in my life. Not until recently did I begin to see Ruth's side. And, John, everyone has their side."

"What could possibly be Vicky's side? She had a baby and couldn't tell me about it."

"But it happened before you two were even dating."

"Yeah, but the woman I fell in love with was living a lie." John surged to his feet, his stance rigid.

"Was she really? She'd done what she thought was best for the child then picked up the pieces of her life and moved on. Granted, she made a mistake not telling you about it, but no one is perfect."

John fisted his hands, his back to Kane.

"You two have a good marriage. Don't throw it away because you're angry. Look what I did. I've thrown the last three years of my life away because of my anger. I haven't moved on since the time I woke up in the hospital and discovered I had lost part of my leg. I drove Ruth away. I isolated myself from everyone. I haven't really been living. Do you want that to happen to you?"

His friend spread his fingers wide. "I want my family the way it was."

"Change happens to us all the time. Often we don't have control over it, but we can control how we deal with it." Kane stood and grasped John's shoulder. "You have the life I want. A loving wife and children. Don't turn your back on it like I did."

Like I'm doing.

The thought stunned Kane. Was that what he was doing by letting Maggie walk out of his life?

"Do you need any help packing?" Edwina asked from the doorway of her spare bedroom late Monday afternoon.

Maggie zipped up her suitcase and then turned toward her friend. "No."

"I don't like the idea of you being in your apartment alone. I don't mind helping."

"I appreciate your offer, but I don't have anything to worry about now. Dr. Johnson is in jail." She grinned. "Besides, Edwina, I'm a big girl. I was going to move out when the apartment was finished."

"I know, but I can't help it if I worry about you. What if Dr. Johnson didn't kill Henry? David says they won't charge him until the DNA tests on the shirt come back. That could take a while."

"I'm gonna be fine." If she said that enough, she might begin to believe that. Right now her heart felt as though it were broken into a hundred pieces, and like Humpty Dumpty, she wasn't sure she could put it back together. "I'm going to get my things over several evenings. I've got some boxes I'll fill tonight and load in my car. I'm glad I had to throw out some of my possessions. Less to pack up. Quit worrying about me."

"Now tell me again why you are leaving. The kids know you are their sister and are thrilled. John hasn't moved out of the apartment upstairs. And you love Kane." She tapped her temple. "I know these things, so you can't deny what you feel for him."

"You just don't want to admit your matchmaking didn't work this time." Maggie strode toward the older woman she'd become quite fond of in a short period of time. "And I won't deny I care—" she shook her head "—no, you're right, love Kane, but it takes two to make a relationship work. I haven't even seen him since yesterday."

"Give him time. He'll come around."

"I don't want him to come around. I want him to accept me with faults and all. If he expects me to be the perfect woman, I've got news for him. I'm not. Never will be." Maggie gave Edwina a hug and then grabbed the boxes by the door. "I won't leave without stopping by and letting you know."

"I've gotten used to having you here. Are you sure you want to stay at the dorm this week?"

"Yes." *Because if I stayed here, seeing Kane would tempt me not to leave.* She couldn't take his continual rejection. She'd fought that her whole life.

With the containers in hand, Maggie headed up to her almost-renovated apartment. As she passed Vicky's door, she smiled at the memory yesterday evening of the hugs she'd received from both Kenny and Ashley. She was determined she would be in their life even from St. Louis. She didn't intend to lose them after finding them. She would take the money Henry had left her and set up a college fund for both Kenny and Ashley as well as some children involved in the Southside Recreational Center. At least some good would come from her inheritance.

In her apartment she scanned the living room she had come to think of as her home in a short time. Where else would she find a place where the people had cared about her, had been so concerned when she'd been attacked?

Her gaze lit upon the mantel, and she saw the leather pouch sticking out from behind a photo of her adoptive father. She'd forgotten about putting it there when David had come to pick up the evidence hidden in that pouch.

She should read the other papers she hadn't at the bank or on the long ride back to Seven Oaks. She wasn't sure she wanted to, but she couldn't leave it here.

Crossing to the mantel, she slid the pouch out from its hiding place and dropped it in the top box. She would start with the kitchen and work her way through the apartment.

When she entered that room and set the containers on the table, her gaze caught sight of the leather pouch, its presence taunting her. If she read its contents now, then she could put it away forever, never to think about Henry Payne again.

She fingered the only thing she hadn't looked at, a sealed envelope with her name sprawled across it as though he had only wanted her to read what was inside. With a deep breath, she tore the end and removed the piece of stationery. Her hands began to tremble as she unfolded the letter.

She had only intended to skim the sheet of paper, but as soon as she started, she found herself immersed in her biological father's explanation. "All I could do was content myself with following your life from afar. I wouldn't disrupt the kind of relationship I saw you had with your adoptive father, but I had wanted that, still do as I write this. Although Vicky denied me the chance to be your father, I don't really blame her. We were too young, and now it's too late. But that doesn't mean I didn't love you." Those words that Henry had written released her sorrow, long bottled up inside her.

Through her tears, the end blurred. She swiped at them and tried to finish reading. But they fell onto the penned letter. She cried for the man who fathered her and had loved her in his own way. She cried for the mistake two teens had made when they had thought they had been in love. She cried for what she wouldn't have—a life with Kane, a family to love.

Finally she wiped her tears from her eyes and perused the rest of the letter. Carefully she folded it and slid it back into its envelope.

Now when she looked around the kitchen, she tried to imagine Henry cooking his meals, a lonely man who had forgotten how to relate to others. It didn't fit with the man she'd come to learn about. A man she was now learning was a series of contradictions.

She put the leather pouch in the box and switched on her MP3 player to drown out all thoughts in the music she loved. She was exhausted from thinking about the past, the future. Using her earplugs, she determinedly turned from the cardboard carton to set about doing the work she had come to do. Quickly she became lost in the classical tunes.

Finished with her kitchen a half hour later, Maggie removed her earplugs and then taped the containers and marked them with numbers. She carried each one to the foyer, where she stacked the boxes. Then she strode toward her bedroom. She paused in the entrance into her office to see what was left to do before Kane could advertise the apartment. Noticing the closet open, she decided to make sure she'd gotten everything salvageable out of it.

She took a few paces toward it when suddenly a figure emerged from it. Her gaze flew to his face. Surprise widened his eyes.

"What are you doing here?" She backed up a step.

He held a hammer and a screwdriver. All surprise fled his

features as resolve fell into place. He moved toward her. Determination and something else—menace—glinted in his gaze.

Maggie whirled around and started for the door. Two feet from it the intruder tackled her to the floor.

THIRTEEN

Kane knocked on Edwina's door. He'd been held up at the university because of all the mess involving Dr. Johnson. He wanted to get home to see Maggie before she left for the dorm.

"She's upstairs in her apartment packing."

"Great. Thanks." He swung around.

"Don't go up there, Kane."

He glanced back at Edwina. "Why not?"

"If you're only going so you can hurt Maggie further, then just leave her alone. She's gone through enough lately."

He smiled. "That's not what I intend to do." He hurried up the stairs.

Bradley pinned Maggie to the hardwood floor, pressing her face into it. "Your father is the reason I'm here," he hissed next to her ear.

Pain from her jaw spread through her. Bradley's weight constricted the rise and fall of her chest. Her lungs began to burn from lack of oxygen.

"Please get up," she managed to whisper. "Can't breathe."

"What do you think it's been like for me these past weeks wondering when you'd find the photos?"

What photos? She wanted to ask that question, but she

didn't have enough breath to. Blackness swirled about the edges of her mind.

A rap sounded from the other room.

Bradley must have jerked around because the pressure on her chest eased some. Air rushed into her lungs for a few blissful seconds, giving Maggie a chance. She started to scream, but only a squeak passed her lips. Bradley settled himself back into place, pressing even harder.

Kane knocked again when Maggie didn't answer her door and waited a good minute. Obviously she didn't want to see him. Maybe he would catch her tomorrow. Maybe she would be ready to listen to him. He began walking toward the staircase. At the top of them, he couldn't take the first step down.

He needed to see her. He'd been wrong, and he had to tell her. If he didn't, he wouldn't be able to sleep. He'd let Ruth walk out of his life because he was angry and afraid. He wasn't going to do that again.

Lord, please help me to get through to her. Help me choose the right words.

Kane strode back to apartment 2A and rapped on the door. When she didn't answer his knock, he couldn't stop his concern from surfacing. With all that had happened in the last month, he had to be sure she was safe. He let himself in. A noise coming from the spare bedroom drew him down the hall. She was probably absorbed in her packing.

"Maggie, it's me."

Hearing Kane's deep voice sent relief through Maggie for a second until she realized he was in danger now, too. A spark of her fighting spirit demanded she do something—anything— to get Bradley off her and alert Kane. She squirmed, bringing her leg up so her heel struck the man in the back.

But before she could do anything else, he lifted himself off her and locked his arms around her, dragging her up and against him. The other hand covered her mouth and nose. The room spun before her. She went limp in his embrace, but he still held her against his front as he hauled her away from the door. Suddenly tension whipped down Bradley's length. Dropping his hand from her mouth, he fumbled for something, then brought the screwdriver up to her left ear.

Across the room Kane stood in the doorway with a calm resolve on his face that glaciated Maggie, the expression of a predator when he'd found his prey and cornered it sculpted his features in intimidation.

"Let her go." The steel in Kane's voice was razor sharp.

"If you come any farther into the room," Bradley said while sticking the screwdriver into her ear, "I won't hesitate to use this. I have nothing to lose now."

Nothing to lose? Did the police have the wrong suspect in Henry's murder case?

"What do you gain by holding Maggie?" A slight narrowing of Kane's eyes spoke volumes of his real feelings.

"All I wanted was the photos. I never intended for anyone to get hurt, but Henry walked in…" He didn't finish his sentence, but Bradley's almost hysterical tone conveyed the sense of a desperate man.

"What photos? Maybe I can help you find them." Kane took a small step forward, his expression and voice composed, even.

"You two found some more stuff that Henry left. I heard about it from David, but you didn't give any photos to him. So where are they?"

"We didn't find anything except the evidence against Dr. Johnson and Maggie's birth certificate." Kane came another foot closer.

"Stay right there. I've got to think. If you didn't find them, then they are still in here somewhere. I've been able to check most of the other rooms pretty thoroughly. This was my last one."

Bradley's hold on her loosened slightly, the screwdriver no longer in her ear. Maggie jabbed her elbow back into his stomach at the same time she went totally limp. She slipped from his loosened embrace.

Kane charged forward, slamming into Bradley. The tool went flying from his grasp, missing Maggie's head by several inches. Kane wrestled the tall, thin man to the floor, sitting on him and pinning Bradley with his forearm across Edwina's nephew's upper chest. Bradley bucked and twisted, a frenzy to his actions.

"Call the police, Maggie."

She scrambled to the phone on the floor near the window and made the call. "David's coming."

Kane thrust his face close to Bradley's. "It's over. You don't have anywhere to hide."

The fight siphoned from her attacker. He sagged back on the floor. "I just wanted to protect her. Everything got out of hand."

Kane eased back some but kept a wary eye and hold on Bradley. "What got out of hand?"

"Two months ago Henry told Beth he could ruin her life at any time he wanted. He couldn't stand to see her happy with me."

Maggie moved forward. "How?" She remembered Henry had told Vicky the same thing.

"He had pictures and a video of her that if they got out she would lose the job she'd finally gotten at the university. Her dream job. I couldn't stand to watch her fret and worry until she was making herself sick. I had to do something to find them. I love her." Bradley buried his face in his hands. "I thought when I didn't find anything that day I broke into the apartment there wasn't any photos. I came back to make sure. Still nothing surfaced. But everything changed when you found the flash drive. I knew he'd done something like that with the photos of Beth and the video he took of her."

"What was on the photos?" Kane kneeled on his right knee.

"She wouldn't tell me. I don't care what they showed. I love her no matter what. I told her that, and all she could do was cry. I can't stand to see her so miserable." Bradley's gaze stabbed Maggie hovering behind Kane. "Your father had a way of destroying people. I wasn't going to let him destroy Beth from the grave."

She squared her shoulders, tilting up her chin. "I'm not responsible for Henry's actions, so quit looking at me as if I am."

Kane rose. "There might not be any photos. Maggie and I checked this apartment thoroughly and never found anything besides those two flash drives."

"Until you found the first one," Bradley said as his glance slipped to her again but this time he banked his anger, "I hadn't thought Henry would put them on a flash drive, but they are perfect for hiding things. They're small. One could be concealed easily."

"What could be easily concealed?" David asked from the doorway.

Maggie spun around, so focused she hadn't heard the detective enter the apartment. "Another flash drive."

David crossed the room and hauled his cousin to his feet. "More incriminating evidence?"

"Something to do with Beth Warren."

"And it led you to break and enter into this apartment? I hope it was important, because I can't get you out of this scrape." David peered at Maggie. "Are you pressing charges?"

She hesitated. Bradley was protecting a woman. He was Edwina's nephew. What if she misunderstood his references to being in Henry's apartment while he was alive? "I…"

"I'm pressing charges." Kane glared at Bradley. "He threatened Maggie and held her captive. He was the one who attacked her the first time. He admitted it. You might not be able to link him to the fire, but he was the one. I'm sure. He had access and motive. And worse, I think he killed Henry. He all but admitted he was in the apartment and Henry walked in on him. He's been frantic to cover everything up. I bet if you check his pockets you'll find evidence on how he got in here."

"Empty your pockets." David withdrew his handcuffs.

Bradley removed his wallet and a set of keys, two new looking.

"May I?" Kane held out his palm for the keys, which David gave him.

While Kane left, limping slightly, David snapped the cuffs on his cousin.

When Kane returned, his frown deepened. "One of those keys fits the new lock on this apartment. I'm sure the other one is to this building. How did you get them?" His lethally quiet voice brooked no argument.

"The one to the building is from my parents. The other, from Edwina. She's easy to distract."

David jerked his cousin toward the door. "How could you do that to Aunt Edwina? She's been so good to you. When the DNA comes back on the shirt, we'll have hard evidence. In the meantime, I'm charging you with breaking and entering and attempted murder." He glanced back at Maggie and Kane. "I'll need you to come down to the station later."

"Gladly," Kane bit out, his hands clutched.

When the pair left, Maggie sank to the floor, her legs threatening to give out on her. She never wanted to step foot in this place again. It was definitely jinxed.

Kane hobbled toward her and offered her his hand. "Let's get some fresh air. This wasn't exactly what I imagined this evening being like."

"What were you imagining?" She fit her palm against his, and he yanked her to a standing position.

A few minutes later when Kane started down the stairs to the basement, she tensed. "Where are we going?" The next to last place she wanted to be was in his apartment—scratch that, the last place.

"Outside. Remember I said fresh air." He arched an eyebrow, a gleam sparkling in his eyes as though he could read her thoughts. "Where did you think I was going?" he asked, way too innocently, as he passed his door and pushed open the one to the backyard.

She refused to say anything. For some reason his mood was light and flirtatious as though the past five days hadn't occurred. It was as if he wasn't furious at her for ruining John and Vicky's marriage, for not telling him who she was.

At the bench by the lake he sat and pulled her down next to him. She started to protest when he said, "We need to talk."

"I'm all out of talking. My head is still reeling from discovering Bradley going through my apartment—apparently again. I thought it was Dr. Johnson, but it was Bradley. I wish it was Dr. Johnson. Poor Edwina and David." She shook her head. "I should have been safe in my own home. I—"

Kane's chuckle cut off her next words. "Maggie, be quiet."

"Well, I've—"

"I'm sorry. Not about the being quiet but about my reaction to the news you were Vicky's daughter. I was wrong. It was between you and Vicky." He released her hand finally, kneading the top of his left thigh.

"Are you hurt?"

"I hit it wrong when I went down. It'll be okay."

"Bradley has a lot to answer for. Terrorizing the whole building, including his parents and aunt."

Kane turned toward her and laid his fingers over her mouth.

"I'm trying to tell you, Maggie Ridgeway, that I care about you. I don't want you to leave Seven Oaks. What's back in St. Louis for you?"

She wanted to tell him peace and quiet, her old life, but she couldn't because neither held much for her at the moment. His words gave her hope. He cared about her. Was that enough? Or would she end up being hurt in the end because he couldn't commit to another totally as she knew she needed?

She bolted from the bench and put some distance between them. "I can't do this. What do you want from me? Why all of a sudden do you want me to stay?"

He plunged his fingers through his hair. "I'm doing a poor job of explaining myself. I've never been good at showing my emotions."

"What emotions?"

"I want you in my life. I need you in my life." His gaze fastened onto hers. "Until you came here, I hadn't been living. I went through the motions only. You made me care again about life. I told the board of directors at the university that I would stay in my position. I don't want to retreat to my workshop."

Her heartbeat increased. She took a step toward him.

He rose. "Before I came up to see you, I prayed for the right words to convince you not to leave. Your family is here now. The kids adore you. John and Vicky will work their marriage out."

But where exactly does that leave us? As much as she wanted to say that question out loud she couldn't. She couldn't go through another rejection. "I can't live here." Especially now that she knew Henry had been her biological father.

An unreadable expression descended on his face, reminding Maggie of how hard it was for Kane to open up to another. He turned as though to leave.

Take the risk, Maggie.

"Kane, don't go."

He glanced back as he eased down onto the bench. "I guess I hit my knee harder than I thought."

Relief fluttered through her. Maggie closed the distance between them and sat next to him. "Maybe you should have a doctor take a look at it."

"Not yet. I don't think I've made myself clear to you. I love you and want to share my life with you. If you can't live here, we can go somewhere else so long as we are together."

His words stunned her. "You love me?"

"What do you think I've been telling you for the past ten minutes?"

"All the reasons to stay in Seven Oaks but that one."

"I know I'm a work in progress, but hopefully you'll think it's worth your effort. I've already started going to my support group. They're helping me handle the loss of my leg. And lately the Lord and I have come to an understanding."

"Oh?" She leaned into him, slipping her arm around his shoulder.

"Yeah. I survived when others didn't, and I promised Him I wouldn't throw that opportunity away. He gave me a second chance, and I almost blew it. Not any longer." Kane took her hand and looked into her eyes. "We'll live wherever you want."

"When I said I couldn't live here, I meant in apartment 2A. It holds too many memories for me. I would love to live anywhere else in Seven Oaks, preferably close to Kenny and Ashley."

"Then you'll marry me?"

"I wouldn't have it any other way. I love you." Wrapping her arms around him, Maggie kissed Kane.

EPILOGUE

When her husband threw himself into something, Kane went all the way. Maggie increased her jogging speed to make up for the fact he had longer legs than she did.

"Let's go by the gazebo at the park. I like that end best," she said, thinking of the surprise she had for him. She'd been so good at keeping it a secret—a secret that would bring joy, not hurt.

"Race you to it." He glanced over at her, grinned, then took off.

She let him go a few paces in front for a few seconds. She never tired of watching him move with the ease of a runner who had used a prosthetic leg his whole life. A year ago he would never have worn shorts. Now he wore them whenever the weather was the slightest bit warm.

He rounded the bend in the path and almost immediately slowed his gait until he came to a halt at the edge of the group of friends assembled for his birthday. He turned toward her as she stopped next to him.

"Was this your idea?"

"Of course. I love throwing parties, and what better excuse than your birthday, old man. Let's see, you're now seven years older than me."

"But not for long." He grabbed her hand and faced the gazebo decorated by Vicky, Kenny and Ashley that morning.

Red, white and blue streamers hung from the latticework while a huge sign proclaimed to the world what day it was. John and David already had the grill going with hamburgers on it. The aroma of meat, mingling with the scent of mowed grass, filled the clearing.

"I can't believe you did this when we've been running," Kane whispered as he moved through the crowd from Twin Oaks and work.

"Look around. Everyone is ready for some fun and games. So a little sweat won't bother anyone. I've planned a few silly ones to get the kids involved."

"I'm almost afraid to ask what."

"The first one involves eggs at Kenny's insistence." Maggie saw her younger brother laughing at something Edwina said. In this past year the troubled child she'd caught glimpses of when she'd first come to Seven Oaks was gone. He would be all right as would Ashley. Thankfully Edwina had recovered from the shock of discovering her nephew killed Henry to protect the woman he loved. DNA evidence had proved it and he'd confessed. And Beth Warren's secret was out—she'd shoplifted to support a drug habit years ago. "And my sister's was a game that involves water balloons."

Kane groaned as Ashley sprinted up to Maggie, tugging on her T-shirt to get her attention. "Can we eat now? Mommy said we had to wait to you all came."

She tousled the little girl's hair. "Sure, and I won't be far behind you. I'm starved."

Kane leaned close to Maggie's ear as Ashley rushed to her mother to let her know. "Have you said anything to them yet about expecting a baby?"

She shook her head. "I only told you this morning. What better present for your birthday!"

"Yeah, the best." Excitement at the fact he would be a father in less than seven months glittered in his eyes. "We could tell everyone now."

"I thought we would at Sunday night dinner at Vicky's. That way it would be just family. After that I thought I would say something to Edwina. Then the whole world would know by the next day."

Kane laughed.

The sound warmed Maggie. Her husband had laughed a lot this past year. She couldn't resist standing on tiptoe and planting a kiss on his mouth.

"Hey, you two, our next president of Seven Oaks University has to be above reproach," Vicky said as she and John joined them.

Kane's eyes widened in surprise. "What are you talking about?"

"I've heard some members of the board of directors discussing who would be good when the interim one steps down at the end of next year. And Kane, you're at the top of everyone's list."

"So that explains the invitation to have lunch with a couple of them next week."

"He really doesn't listen to the gossip flying around the university, does he?" Vicky asked Maggie.

"Probably because he's been so caught up in the renovation of our home. We're determined to have it completed by the end of summer. I hate living in chaos."

"But being down the street from Twin Oaks has been wonderful. The kids love going over to your house and helping."

"Kane," John said and slapped Kane on the back, "I think the talk is gonna turn to women stuff. Want to join me at the food table?"

The second the men disappeared in the group Vicky pulled Maggie away from the others. "I know you haven't said anything yet, but when is the baby due?"

"Baby?"

"A mother can tell. Besides, Kenny said something about you having to go to the doctor the other day. Well?"

"The end of November."

Vicky let out a shrill of delight and hugged her. "I'm going to be a grandmother!"

* * * * *

Dear Reader,

This story is about forgiveness and guilt. I often return to these themes in my stories. Guilt drives people to do all kinds of different things—from cutting themselves off from others (like Kane) to being afraid a secret will be revealed (like Vicky and several other characters in *Poisoned Secrets*). But my main theme is about forgiveness, which Maggie had to deal with. She had a lot of anger built up toward her birth mother that had to be resolved before she could move on. I hope you enjoyed their journey toward a richer life.

I love hearing from readers. You can contact me at margaretdaley@gmail.com, or at P.O. Box 2074, Tulsa, OK 74101. You can also learn more about my books at www.margaretdaley.com. I have a quarterly newsletter that you can sign up for, or you can enter my monthly drawings by signing my guest book on the Web site.

Best wishes,

Margaret Daley

DISCUSSION QUESTIONS

1. Is there someone in your life you've been able to forgive? What did they do to you? What made you forgive him or her?

2. Do you have someone who can't forgive you? Why?

3. How did the Lord handle forgiveness when someone sinned against Him?

4. Have you ever kept a secret that if revealed would harm someone? Did it come out anyway?

5. Kane had trouble dealing with his disability. Has this happened to you or a loved one? How can that person be helped?

6. Who is your favorite character? Why?

7. What is your favorite scene? Why?

8. Maggie observed life from the outside looking in. How do you look at life and interact with others? Does your faith influence that interaction?

9. Vicky made a mistake when she was a teenager. It came back to haunt her. Has this happened to you? How did you handle it?

10. Did you figure out who killed Henry? What led you to the murderer?

11. Maggie talked with the Lord often, like a one-sided conversation. How do you interact with Him?

12. Bradley did something stupid that snowballed and got out of hand. Have you ever had that happen to you? How did it turn out? Were you able to fix it? How?

Turn the page for a sneak preview of bestselling author
Jillian Hart's novella
"Finally a Family"

One of two heartwarming stories celebrating motherhood in
IN A MOTHER'S ARMS

On sale April 2009, only from Steeple Hill Love Inspired
Historical.

Montana Territory, 1884

Molly McKaslin sat in her rocking chair in her cozy little shanty with her favorite book in hand. The lush new-spring green of the Montana prairie spread out before her like a painting, framed by the wooden window. The blue sky was without a single cloud to mar it. Lemony sunshine spilled over the land and across the open window's sill. The door was wedged open, letting the outside noises in—the snap of laundry on the clothesline and the chomping crunch of an animal grazing. My, it sounded terribly close.

The peaceful afternoon quiet shattered with a crash. She leaped to her feet to see her good—and only—china vase splintered on the newly washed wood floor. She stared in shock at the culprit standing at her other window. A golden cow with a white blaze down her face poked her head farther across the sill. The bovine gave a woeful moo. One look told her this was the only animal in the yard.

"And just what are you doing out on your own?" She set her book aside.

The cow lowed again. She was a small heifer, still probably more baby than adult. The cow lunged against the sill, straining toward the cookie racks on the table.

"At least I know how to catch you." She grabbed a cookie off the rack and the heifer's eyes widened. "I don't recognize you, so I don't think you belong here."

Molly skirted around the mess on the floor and headed toward the door. This was the consequence of agreeing to live in the country, when she had vowed never to do so again. But her path had led her to this opportunity, living on her cousin's land and helping the family. God had quite a sense of humor, indeed.

Before she could take two steps into the soft, lush grass surrounding her shanty, the cow came running, head down, big brown eyes fastened on the cookie. The ground shook.

Uh-oh. Molly's heart skipped two beats.

"No, Sukie, no!" High, girlish voices carried on the wind.

Molly briefly caught sight of two identical school-aged girls racing down the long dirt road. The animal was too single-minded to respond. She pounded the final few yards, her gaze fixed on the cookie.

"Stop, Sukie. Whoa." Molly kept her voice low and kindly firm. She knew cows responded to kindness better than to anything else. She also knew they were not good at stopping, so she dropped the cookie on the ground and neatly stepped out of the way. The cow skidded well past the cookie and the place where Molly had been standing.

"It's right here." She showed the cow where the oatmeal treat was resting in the clean grass. While the animal backed up and nipped up the goody, Molly grabbed the cow's rope halter.

"Good. She didn't stomp you into bits," one of the girls said in serious relief. "She ran me over real good just last week."

"We thought you were a goner," the second girl said. "She's real nice, but she doesn't see very well."

"She sees well enough to have found me." Molly studied the girls. They both had identical black braids and golden-hazel eyes and fine-boned porcelain faces. One twin wore a green calico dress with matching sunbonnet, while the other wore blue. She recognized the girls from church and around town. "Aren't you the doctor's children?"

"Yep, that's us." The first girl offered a beaming, dimpled

smile. "I'm Penelope and that's Prudence. We're real glad you found Sukie."

"We wouldn't want a cougar to get her."

"Or a bear."

What adorable children. A faint scattering of freckles dappled across their sun-kissed noses, and there was glint of trouble in their eyes as the twins looked at one another. The place in her soul thirsty for a child of her own ached painfully. She felt hollow and empty, as if her body would always remember carrying the baby she had lost. For one moment it was as if the wind died and the earth vanished.

"Hey, what is she eating?" One of the girls tumbled forward. "It smells like a cookie. You are a bad girl, Sukie."

"Did she walk into your house and eat off the counter?" Penelope wanted to know.

The grass crinkled beneath her feet as the cow tugged her toward the girls. "No, she went through the window."

Penelope went up on tiptoe. "I see them. They look real good."

Molly gazed down at their sweet and innocent faces. She wasn't fooled. Then again, she was a soft touch. "I'll see what I can do."

She headed back inside. "Do you girls need help getting the cow home?"

"No. She's real tame." Penelope and the cow trailed after her, hesitating outside the door. "We can lead her anywhere."

"Yeah, she only runs off when she's looking for us."

"Thank you so much, Mrs.—" Penelope took the napkin-wrapped stack of cookies. "We don't know your name."

"This is the McKaslin ranch," Prudence said thoughtfully. "But I know you're not Mrs. McKaslin."

"I'm the cousin. I moved here this last winter. You can call me Molly."

Penelope gave her twin a cookie. Beneath the brim of her sunbonnet, her face crinkled with serious thought. "You don't know our pa yet?"

"No, I only know Dr. Frost by reputation. I hear he's a fine doctor." That was all she knew. Of course she had seen his fancy black buggy speeding down the country roads at all hours. Sometimes she caught a brief sight of the man driving as the horse-drawn vehicle passed—an impression of a black Stetson, a strong granite profile and impressively wide shoulders.

Although she was on her own and free to marry, she paid little heed to eligible men. All she knew of Dr. Sam Frost was that he was a widower and a father and a faithful man, for he often appeared very serious in church. She reached through the open door to where her coats hung on wall pegs and worked the sash off her winter wool.

Prudence smiled. "Our pa's real nice and you make good cookies."

"And you're real pretty." Penelope was so excited she didn't notice Sukie stealing her cookie. "Do you like Pa?"

"I don't know the man, so I can't like him. I suppose I can't dislike him either." She bent to secure the sash around Sukie's halter. "Let me walk you girls across the road."

"You ought to come home with us." Penelope grinned. "Then you can meet Pa."

"Do you want to get married?" Penelope's feet were planted.

So were Prudence's. "Yes! You could marry Pa. Do you want to?"

"M-marry your pa?" Shock splashed over her like icy water.

"Sure. You could be our ma."

"And then Pa wouldn't be so lonely anymore."

Molly blinked. The words were starting to sink in. The poor girls, wishing so much for a mother that they would take any stranger who was kind to them. "No, I certainly cannot marry a perfect stranger, but thank you for asking. I would take you two in a heartbeat."

"You would?" Penelope looked surprised. "Really?"

"We're an awful lot of trouble. Our housekeeper said that three times today since church."

"Does your pa know you propose on his behalf?"

"Now he does," a deep baritone answered. Dr. Frost marched into sight, rounding the corner of the shanty. His hat brim shaded his face, casting shadows across his chiseled features, giving him an even more imposing appearance. "Girls! Home! Not another word."

"But we had to save Sukie."

"She could have been eaten by a wolf."

Molly watched the good doctor's mouth twitch. She couldn't be sure, but a flash of humor could have twinkled in the depths of his eyes.

"You must be the cousin." He swept off his hat. The twinkle faded from his eyes and the hint of a grin from his lips. It was clear that while his daughters amused him, she did not. "I had no idea you would be so young."

"And pretty," Penelope, obviously the troublemaker, added mischievously.

Molly's face heated. The poor girl must need glasses. Although Molly was still young, time and sadness had made its mark on her. The imposing man had turned into granite as he faced her. Of course he had overheard his daughters' proposal, so that might explain it.

She smiled and took a step away from him. "Dr. Frost, I'm glad you found your daughters. I was about ready to bring them back to you."

"I'll save you the trouble." He didn't look happy. "Girls, take that cow home. I need to stay and apologize to Miss McKaslin."

She was a "Mrs." but she didn't correct him. She had put away her black dresses and her grief. Her marriage had mostly been a long string of broken dreams. She did better when she didn't remember. "Please don't be too hard on the girls on my behalf. Sukie's arrival livened up my day."

"At least there was no harm done." He winced. "There was harm? What happened?"

"I didn't say a word."

"No, but I could see it on your face."

Had he been watching her so closely? Or had she been so unguarded? Perhaps it was his closeness. She could see bronze flecks in his gold eyes, and smell the scents of soap and spring clinging to his shirt. A spark of awareness snapped within her like a candle newly lit. "It was a vase. Sukie knocked it off my windowsill when she tried to eat the flowers, but it was an accident."

"The girls should take better care of their pet." He drew his broad shoulders into an unyielding line. He turned to check on the twins, who were progressing down the road. The wind ruffled his dark hair. He seemed distant. Lost. "How much was the vase worth?"

How did she tell him it was without price? Perhaps it would be best not to open that door to her heart. "It was simply a vase."

"No, it was more." He stared at his hat clutched in both hands. "Was it a gift?"

"No, it was my mother's."

"And is she gone?"

"Yes."

"Then I cannot pay you its true value. I'm sorry." His gaze met hers with startling intimacy. Perhaps a door was open to his heart as well, because sadness tilted his eyes. He looked like a man with many regrets.

She knew well the weight of that burden. "Please, don't worry about it."

"The girls will replace it." His tone brooked no argument, but it wasn't harsh. "About what my daughters said to you."

"Do you mean their proposal? Don't worry. It's plain to see they are simply children longing for a mother's love."

"Thank you for understanding. Not many folks do."

"Maybe it's because I know something about longing. Life never turns out the way you plan it."

"No. Life can hand you more sorrow than you can carry." Although he did not move a muscle, he appeared changed. Stronger, somehow. Greater. "I'm sorry the girls troubled you, Miss McKaslin."

Mrs., but again she didn't correct him. It was the sorrow she carried that stopped her from it. She preferred to stand in the present with sunlight on her face. "It was a pleasure, Dr. Frost. What blessings you have in those girls."

"That I know." He tipped his hat to her, perhaps a nod of respect, and left her alone with the restless wind and the door still open in her heart.

* * * * *

Don't miss IN A MOTHER'S ARMS
featuring two brand-new novellas from bestselling authors
Jillian Hart and Victoria Bylin.
Available April 2009
from Steeple Hill Love Inspired Historical.

And be sure to look for SPRING CREEK BRIDE
by Janice Thompson,
also available in April 2009.

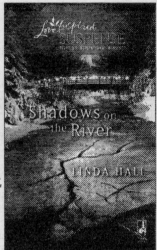

REQUEST YOUR FREE BOOKS!

2 FREE RIVETING INSPIRATIONAL NOVELS
PLUS 2 FREE MYSTERY GIFTS

Love Inspired®
SUSPENSE

YES! Please send me 2 FREE Love Inspired® Suspense novels and my 2 FREE mystery gifts (gifts are worth about $10). After receiving them, if I don't wish to receive any more books, I can return the shipping statement marked "cancel". If I don't cancel, I will receive 4 brand-new novels every month and be billed just $4.24 per book in the U.S. or $4.74 per book in Canada, plus 25¢ shipping and handling per book and applicable taxes, if any*. That's a savings of over 20% off the cover price! I understand that accepting the 2 free books and gifts places me under no obligation to buy anything. I can always return a shipment and cancel at any time. Even if I never buy another book, the two free books and gifts are mine to keep forever.

123 IDN ERXX 323 IDN ERXM

Name	(PLEASE PRINT)	
Address		Apt. #
City	State/Prov.	Zip/Postal Code

Signature (if under 18, a parent or guardian must sign)

Order online at www.LoveInspiredSuspense.com
Or mail to Steeple Hill Reader Service:
IN U.S.A.: P.O. Box 1867, Buffalo, NY 14240-1867
IN CANADA: P.O. Box 609, Fort Erie, Ontario L2A 5X3

Not valid to current subscribers of Love Inspired Suspense books.

Want to try two free books from another series?
Call 1-800-873-8635 or visit www.morefreebooks.com

* Terms and prices subject to change without notice. N.Y. residents add applicable sales tax. Canadian residents will be charged applicable provincial taxes and GST. Offer not valid in Quebec. This offer is limited to one order per household. All orders subject to approval. Credit or debit balances in a customer's account(s) may be offset by any other outstanding balance owed by or to the customer. Please allow 4 to 6 weeks for delivery. Offer available while quantities last.

Your Privacy: Steeple Hill Books is committed to protecting your privacy. Our Privacy Policy is available online at www.SteepleHill.com or upon request from the Reader Service. From time to time we make our lists of customers available to reputable third parties who may have a product or service of interest to you. If you would prefer we not share your name and address, please check here. ☐

LISUS08R

Love Inspired® SUSPENSE

TITLES AVAILABLE NEXT MONTH

On sale April 14, 2009

CODE OF HONOR by Lenora Worth

Get in, save the girl and get back out. CHAIM agent Brice Whelan's agenda seems foolproof...until he tries to rescue missionary/nurse Selena Carter. When danger follows Selena home, Brice has to protect her, which means sticking by her side—whether she wants him there or not.

CLOUD OF SUSPICION by Patricia Davids

Without a Trace

Leather-jacketed rebel Patrick Rivers has always had a bad reputation. And now that he's back in town to settle his stepfather's estate, Patrick knows he isn't welcome. But the chance to keep Shelby Mason safe could be reason enough to stay.

MURDER AT EAGLE SUMMIT by Virginia Smith

A body found on the slopes turns the wedding guests at Eagle Summit ski resort into suspects. Liz Carmichael might be a witness, so she files a police report...with her ex-fiancé, Deputy Tim Richards. After three years apart, she can finally make things right—unless the killer finds her first.

SHADOWS ON THE RIVER by Linda Hall

Ally Roarke was fourteen when she witnessed a murder... and was forced out of town by the teenage killer's prominent parents. Years later, the killer is a respected businessman. And Ally, now a single mom, can't let the past go. Especially when there's another death close to home.